Visible, Invisible and Beyond

A Novel

Tulip Chowdhury

Note: The concept of the spiritual world in this book does not reflect a particular religious belief, nor does it support or oppose any. The visible world also depicts imagined characters.

Visible, Invisible, and Beyond

Copyright © 2013 Tulip Chowdhury

All rights reserved.

ISBN-13: 9781492278726
ISBN-10: 1492278726

Dedicated to my princess, Proma

Part One

Entry of a Soul

one

In the invisible spiritual world a miracle is taking place. Here the Creator is creating life, making souls for living things on Earth, including humans. The heart, a piece of flesh inside each and every human, beats while the soul is there and stops when the soul is taken away. Beyond this invisible world is the Land of Illumination, yet another invisible world. This is the home of all souls. Here are souls ready to journey to the world of the humans and souls returning after their humans die. Life on Earth is a temporary existence for the souls. They tell each other, "Humans borrow souls from our world."

In the Creator's world, the Giver of Life is about to release a human soul into a female human being. This is just one of the Creator's countless creations, turning the invisible into the visible. Mountains, seas, deserts, and plains—all have come from the invisible. In fact the universe and everything beyond come from a state of nothingness.

After the Creator creates the soul, it will be released inside the womb of a woman for a predestined time. Then it will emerge as an addition to mankind, another human added to the ranks of these superior creations with intelligence. For the entry of this soul, the Creator has brought a man and woman together.

An immigrant from Bangladesh, Tareq Khan holds his American wife Daisy close to his bosom where she purrs like a happy cat, snuggling into the hairy muscled chest that she so loves. His hands run up and down her soft, abundantly curved body. His fingers tickle her playfully in places he knows will awake her emotions all the more. In response her delicate hands start caressing him. Their clothes have been thrown all around the bed, and in their perfectly natural state, they blend into each other. The small cozy bedroom contains a lavender scented candle, a fragrance that holds romance for the man and the woman. The candlelight throws shadows, which dance around on the walls. Tareq and Daisy press closer, as if having their hearts beating against each other is not enough. Holding on tighter, almost squeezing his wife, Tareq whispers to Daisy, "Tonight shall be our night of celebration. Without any precautions, today we may be opening the door for that sweet baby we have so long dreamed of."

Daisy's soft blond hair tickles his bare chest, and he lifts her beautiful face to kiss those full lips set beneath bright blue eyes. In the night light, her blue eyes and his dark ones meet. They stare for a long while without blinking, love swimming between their held gazes. As his tanned body meets her delicate white one, it is like the blending of the dark night on the blue sky. They would be meaningless without each other. With bodies entwined, Daisy plays with his hair with her fingers and replies, "I love you, Tareq, more than I can ever say. Perhaps when our child comes, I will find my words with his or her laughter and smiles, for that will be the fruit of our love."

With gentle hands she brings his head to her bosom, and tinkles of laughter escape her as he playfully kisses the gentle rise and fall of her breasts.

"Tareq, this is a special night. I have a feeling that our baby is coming." Daisy whispers over his hair, still playing with his locks.

She loves this man from a strange, faraway land. Yet how deeply they share their love! Indeed love has strange ways of entering life. Tareq, with his manly features, tall frame, and tanned skin, embodies a sweetness that radiates purity. His wide generous mouth set beneath a sharp nose and dreamy eyes makes Daisy catch her breath every time she looks at him. Daisy thinks she is blessed to have him with his gentleness and complete acceptance of her as she is. And she, the young American woman with a body that could put even Venus to shame, has left her home for him. She left her parents when they did not consent to her marrying Tareq.

Looking at Daisy's sharp nose, full lips, blond hair, and blue eyes in the dim light, Tareq says, "You are my mermaid, my fairy and my angel. And I'm even going to have a baby with this unique woman!"

Daisy clings to Tareq when he takes her, as if holding tightly to their dreams, and then they are like one body, sharing passion at its greatest height. The night's silence is broken by their heavy breathing, kisses, and soft whispers of "I love you," over and over. Then finally they lie quietly, spent from the delightful union of their bodies. Outside the crickets drone on in the warm summer night in Fayetteville, North Carolina.

As Tareq and Daisy fall asleep in each other's arms, their dream of having a baby is coming true. The soul is on its way from the Creator. Angels, invisible much like the souls, hover above the happy couple. At times they may take the shape of a man or woman, but on this night they cannot be seen by the people they are working on. They are responsible for delivering the souls when a new life is sent into the world. They also take the souls back to the Creator when a human dies.

Up above, one watchful angel says, "Can't the whole process of making souls be done on Earth? Why make them invisible when their ultimate destination is in the human world, where they are presented with so many interesting appearances? Some humans have small eyes, some have larger ones. Some are tall and some short, and they come with different skin and hair colors too."

"These human souls are complex creations. They have to be taken to definite places on Earth, to be given definite identities!" exclaims another angel standing nearby. He seems to be very worried about the life awaiting this new soul.

The angels ready to descend with the new soul on the Creator's order reply, "Here lies the magic. It is the Creator's will. He sends them, makes them play games of life, and takes them back again. Humans have challenging times on Earth, keeping in mind that from the invisible they come and to the invisible they go. Life on Earth is only a transition. Yet, they get caught with a sense of false permanency as they pursue happiness."

"What is this thing called *happiness*?" asks an angel sitting and watching all that is happening.

Two angels, waiting for the final command to come from the Creator to release the soul, give heavenly smiles and say, "Happiness sits inside each and every human being, waiting to be found. But happiness does not reside alone; it exists with its companion, called *sadness*. Humans shake hands with happiness while on guard, knowing that sadness may soon strike. Actually the ball lies in the hands of the Creator. He winds and rewinds the threads of life. When humans accept this truth and bow down to the superior power that controls their life, they find it easier to accept the ups and downs of life. It also gives them a better insight to happiness."

In the human world, the angels hovering over sleeping Tareq and Daisy wonder what is going on up above in the Creator's world. They made the man and woman meet, but the soul is still not here. There is a time for the sperm and the egg to meet and the fetus to start its life. The angels need the soul to come and enter the new life just when all these happenings align. While the other angels go on debating and wondering about human lives, two angels descend on the small house of Tareq and Daisy on Earth. Upon the command of the Creator, one of them carries the new soul that is to be released into the womb of Daisy. The summer night is deliciously warm. Together the angels nudge the fluttering soul forward as it is released into Daisy. It is ready for its human abode.

The angels smile tenderly as they witness Tareq and Daisy reach out to each other in the deep night. It is as if even in their sleep they feel the soul's entry into their world. Outside the moon spreads its silvery light on the dark forms of the trees.

Unknown to the man and woman, many nocturnal beings, along with the moonlight and the wind, are excited to see the angels carrying the soul. They rejoice at every birth. From the spiritual world, the Creator and angels watch as the hearts, minds, and bodies of the man and the woman blend into each other.

"Tareq, Oh, Tareq!" Daisy calls to her love in her sleep.

"Darling, I am with you," he says as he enfolds her soft body in his arms.

The angels smile. Love comes to two hearts with the Creator's wish, and out of this love is new life. A sense of fulfillment that words cannot describe passes between the angels.

Tareq and Daisy snore away, their arms tangled around each other. They are drowning in the sweetness of love while the angels give dreams of a baby.

The intensity of this physical union between the man and woman is destined by the Giver of Life so that the soul will find its place when it flows into the woman's body. Thus, the new soul starts life, growing into a baby in its mother's womb.

Tareq and Daisy look peaceful, with little knowledge of all that has just happened in the invisible world. The angels fly back to their own world, having completed their sacred duty. They have to bring down new souls, for so many babies are born every day in the world of the humans.

Part Two

Souls in the Land of Illumination

two

Like life on Earth, life in the spiritual world also flows like an eternal spring. The souls move around, mingling with other invisible beings. The humans do not try to enter the Land of Illumination, for the Creator keeps this world hidden from them. But if a soul requests for its host to be shown into this land, then a human may be brought to this invisible land in a dream. This is a rare gift the Creator gives to a soul when the host, guided by the soul, reaches complete purity of the heart and mind. And this is how this story of the invisible world is being revealed, getting it written down: upon a soul's request to the Creator for its writer host.

In the Land of Illumination, baffled souls ask each other, "Why does the Giver of Life play these games? He creates the souls, sends them to Earth, and yet then he makes sure to bring them back to his invisible world."

One particularly wise soul, made ready by the Creator to lead masses of people in the human world, smiles and says, "The game of life the Creator plays has one word. It is 'borphilo-livphilo-gophilo-nat' in our world of the souls. Humans spend their whole lives searching for words to describe the exact meaning of life but cannot. They are forced to hold life with debated meanings, but this one word, like many secrets of life, is hidden from the humans."

"Phew!" says the soul of a man studying ancient philosophy in preparation for his future host, a professor. "That certainly is a big word! I haven't come across anything like it in the human vocabulary."

The wise soul explains, "*Philo* refers to the humans' deepest emotion—love. So, breaking it down, it means something like 'born with love, live with love, or die with love.' *Nat* joins the bounties in nature. The Creator's message to humans is to love all. It is like the magic solution to the meaning of life. Love brings good over evil, and it is goodness that the Creator seeks in his unique creation, mankind. The Creator also expresses the need to protect nature outside. *Nat* also speaks for the biological being of the human body, the natural way of the body in its growth and decay. To be natural in something is the basic ingredient of life."

As if to express the importance of nature, the Creator has blessed the Land of Illumination with trees, colorful flowers, and tranquil lakes. There is an image of serenity and peace that seems to breathe here eternally. Unlike the invisible inhabitants of this land, all of nature's bounties are visible. Birds, butterflies, and bees playing around the trees make this land look like an enchanted place. In this land also live the genies. They fly around the Land of Illumination, Heaven, Earth, and the universe. They are often with human beings on Earth and are well versed in the countless challenges of human life.

A soul standing quietly is confused while listening to the ongoing discourse on human lives. She asks a genie just flown in, "Since the Creator will stop the heart and bring the soul back, why are they sent to the human beings and asked to help them get worldly goods? Why give them this false dream of possessing life's blessings permanently? In this game of life, what do the humans call us, anyway?"

The genie settling down on the branch of a tree, chuckles and says, "Of the Creator's doings, how little we know! Without their attraction to worldly needs, a human's life would be like a meaningless journey. But the journey is based on strict rules of right and wrong, and that is where they often get lost. Humans know that you souls are life for them. In your world you are called 'Dancing Lights.' They call you the 'soul.' When the souls leave after human beings die, they are then called 'spirits' by the humans. A spirit can take shape of another deceased person when directed by the Creator." The genie pauses and takes a look around, as if to make sure that she has the attention of the confused souls around her.

She sighs when she finds the souls staring at her balefully and ends her sermon. "These spirits can go to the human world, but they are usually invisible in their forms. They move upon the Creator's will, and so at times they can be seen too by humans for special moments related to love, hate or divine revelations."

Silently the souls watch the genie as she gets up from her place and suddenly starts flying away. It seems as if she were there just to impart her knowledge of the Creator's creations.

The Creator with His omnipresence is busy in the invisible world and with life on Earth. In the human world with his countless creations, He plays with multitudes of colors, sounds, shapes, emotions, and other things beyond imagination. Humans spend lifetimes discovering the creations of the Creator and often die knowing that they have but known only a fraction. Here again the Creator has bestowed the souls with a unique gift: they can time travel when they need to help their hosts in acquiring knowledge about life. Time traveling requires the Creator's permission, but souls can look into the past or the future when something crucial hangs in the balance.

To touch souls with the vivacity of life, the Creator surrounds them with blossoming verdant nature. To prepare souls for travel to the visible world, the Creator gives them the essence of this life while in the Land of Illumination. He creates countless flowers, all blooming continuously within fractions of seconds. Rivers and lakes flow as birds sing endlessly. Here nights and days blend, and birds need not fly to their nests before sunsets. Angels, spirits, genies, and souls are pulsating with their own lives, and yet there is a mystic silence pregnant with a tranquility of its own.

The angels are here, the embodiment of goodness, kindness, empathy, and all other words humans have discovered to describe love in its best forms. The Creator sends them where He wills. They sometimes come in the form of humans to help other humans.

In this spiritual world, the Creator is endlessly perfecting souls to be placed into the unborn. He only says, "Be!" and a life springs into being. With the flow of time, as He goes through his miracles of developing souls, He has to update them too. He retrieves genes of particular ancestors and places these genes into the soul. This is his way of linking mankind to their past generations.

three

At times the Creator voices his thoughts to the souls he makes. At this moment, He tells the soul in hand, "Because you have to keep the human races connected through genes, your personality traits will blend with those of future generations. I have to put in hard work to make you amenable to technology and at the same time have you hold on to love and compassion for all."

As lust for life is put into humans, their materialistic wants take over. "Give me power! Give me money, houses, cars, and fame!" cry the humans to the Creator. When they go astray in search of worldly goods, the Creator brings them lights through loss or pain, so that they may understand the value of that which they are already blessed. He loves his creations and tries to bring peace to their hearts. He ties a knot on greediness and puts a warning to the souls to guard the hearts against it.

Many souls waiting to go to the human world tremble as the Creator's messages filter down to them. They do not come in a clear voice, and yet the souls hear His words loud and clear.

"Guard the heart. It can destroy, and it can take life to glorious heights. For often the heart loses touch with reason and works only on passion. Touches of love will keep your compassion alive, no matter how strong the greediness grows. Send in vibrations to warn them about where to draw the line. Let it be known that I reward good intentions, even when they fail in their ways. It is the inner being that I see."

The souls waiting to go the human world look worried, and they chant, "We are scared of the fast changing world on Earth. Do we have to go?"

Again they hear the divine message. "Yes, you have to go while the human race thrives. I've blessed humans with intelligence to acquire knowledge. Intoxicated with the power of science, humans are becoming frantic to maximize their worldly work within their limited time. I'm modeling you to adjust to the age of the Internet and social media, which are revolutionizing the human world. I also empower a part of the brain with the ability to adjust, so you souls will balance the brains and the hearts while the humans venture into the endless power of science."

Just then an angel flies in among the souls. The Creator has called him for a report on the activities of Earth. In a frustrated voice, this angel says, "My Lord, how am I to take care of the new breeds of human beings? They are so tempted in life by luxury and the use of automatic machines and the thousands of things that make life easier. The needy find happiness in simple things, but those who have wealth are the ones difficult to keep track of."

The Creator is silent for a while before sending his message to the souls. "When your hosts engage or even begin to think of wrongdoing, give them premonitions of their inevitable deaths, make them feel suffocated—the whole body is to get a sick feeling, so that they may think twice. Genies, angels, and spirits of the dead are allowed to visit the human world when I think they can help a person. I have also given souls the power to time travel when needed for the welfare of their hosts. But let your hosts know that I respond to them when they remember me and call for my help."

Another angel sitting near a bed of white flowers says, "It is a strange game you play, Creator. You send mankind and yet create countless alluring puzzles in their everyday lives."

"Ah, indeed, my reasons are known to me only!" the Creator states.

While making the souls, the Creator also prepares places for souls that will go to the illiterate masses, people who are not yet aware of the immense possibilities life holds for them. He keeps those souls ready to accept a world with lesser blessings. While the Creator goes on creating unique lives, in the Land of Illumination the souls socialize in their own ways. They look after each other, enjoy the community of the spirits and learn about life on Earth from souls that have returned after their hosts die. Yet they remain alert for each command the Giver of Life bestows on them.

The souls have heard of the human species that click away on keyboards to connect to the other sides of Earth via the Internet. The returning souls fill in the gossip line. They have heard that humans even create copies of life, calling it "cloning." The clones may look the same, but the heart cannot be directed without the Creator's will. Love and ethics do not work there. The seat of the clone's heart finds no connection with the souls in the Land of Illumination.

The Creator has given intelligence to humans, and the souls have to balance their intellectual strides in their hosts. So while creating new souls, the Creator adds extra doses of compassion, honesty, patience, and virtue to them. These qualities work like a softener to the walls of fame and money that humans build around them.

One spirit tells the souls, "Within all the Creator's special touches is that touch of compassion without which human beings would be like stones. Love can heal, and love can kill."

The souls are apprehensive about how their hosts will fall in love and how they will guide them about that mysterious element of life on Earth.

A soul who has as of yet not said anything, whispers, "I hope the human I am assigned to will be is happy in love like Tareq and Daisy. I know they are having a baby, and I wonder how the soul in the new life will fare."

A spirit, back to the Land of Illumination after her host died has been listening to the souls. She flutters in the middle of the gathering and remarks, "Happy or sad in life, all people suffer immensely when they have to die and leave their loved ones. Maybe you souls can put a bit of peace in the people that are left behind. They have a terrible time grieving, and we have to make so many trips to stand beside them. But at times I feel happy when people in love call the spirits of their loved ones to witness happiness; those are trips of pleasure. But be careful, souls are not to fall in love with other souls, even as they create great romances for their hosts."

The souls look at each other confused, and then together they exclaim, "Love is divine, but we are not to fall in love?"

The spirit nods wisely awhile and says, "Maybe that is because if allowed to fall in love, you would think more of your own interests than that of your hosts." After a short pause, she continues, saying, "Oh dear, there is the Creator dispatching me to someone. This woman is getting married and wishes her deceased mother to see her husband. I'm to represent her mother."

Watching the spirit float away, the souls wonder how the mother died. The souls give life to the humans, and so thoughts of death send shivers to them, much like those of human beings. The bonding of the souls with their hosts surpasses all other forms of attachments in the human world.

Part Three

Souls in the Buffer Zone

four

Daisy and Tareq sit on the deck of their house. It is Saturday, and after the previous night's intense lovemaking, they are content and relaxed for the weekend. Both have showered, and Daisy's wet hair clings around her beautiful face. Tareq lifts a lock of hair from her eyes as she takes sips from her mug of tea. The garden below them is full of weeds, and the surrounding trees need trimming. Tareq did not have the time in the last few weeks to work in the garden. Some roses and chrysanthemums are braving the tall grasses that are growing with pleasure in the absence of human hands to keep them at bay.

If pregnant, Daisy is supposed to be having the symptoms after some weeks of their marked night. But intuition seems to be working more and the excitements of attaining motherhood is already flooding her heart. Perhaps it is like the tremors of a volcano before it erupts. Unique is the union of a mother and a child, the magnificence of two souls sharing the same host is a wonder beyond words! Daisy's whole being seems to be soaring towards rainbows of thousand colors, climbing heights of ecstasy never experienced before.

Daisy and Tareq are quiet as they share jam and toast. Having all these strange feelings Daisy asks, "Darling, do you think we really did make something last night? Did I conceive, really? I feel as if I am new today."

Tareq takes her left hand and kisses the wedding ring on it, smiling with that wide generous mouth of his. He says softly,

"Who knows? Perhaps we are becoming Papa and Mama and a revolution is taking place in our future."

And true to his words, in the Land of Illumination the souls are busy with hot discussions of human lives while the new life in Daisy flutters like the delicate wings of a butterfly. The angels, souls, conscience, and spirits are having seesaw rides. The angels always caution the entering souls, "Soul, body, mind, and heart: they sit on each life as if balancing the seesaw. When one goes up, the other goes down. They think they are in balance at times, but actually it's the seesaw ride of life. There is a midway where you must hold it all."

Life on Earth amazes the souls as they learn more and more about it. Life comes and goes, think what you want. Reproduction is the master key to all living beings on Earth. Sexual or asexual reproduction is life's own way of continuing life.

The souls are busy too, trying to gain knowledge of the world they will live in while they are with the humans. One soul is puzzled about a new aspect of human life, women having two or three babies at the same time. Bewildered, she asks the Creator, "These days women have twins and triplets more than ever before. They are born together, but do they share a common soul?"

The Creator encourages sharing, but on this issue of blessing mankind with souls, he sends this message: "Each human comes with his or her own soul, be they twins or quadruplets. They come alone and will die alone."

Yet the Creator keeps one firm rule in the making of a human body. In each body, the heart and mind must reason with the soul and make their existence into a blessed world. If they lack harmony the world becomes chaos. The humans' ability to choose between good and evil puts the conscience in stride for satisfaction of the soul. And so the conscience, when in its right place, can motivate the heart and mind to work for the best and keep the soul going strong.

Beyond the flesh, bone, blood, muscle, and all else that makes up human beings, the soul exists. Encased in the body, yet they remain fragile. They vanish on a second's summon from the Creator. Yet souls are the essence of life for all living beings on Earth. Other living things have souls, but human souls have to account for their deeds with the Creator. The souls that get waylaid with the heart and mind feel tremendous pain as they carry on life. After their hosts die, they return to the Creator and their failures set them apart from the other souls who have remained steadfast on the path of goodness.

Birth, life, and death: the soul goes through it all, yet it remains invisible to the naked eye. You feel it, hear it in a loved one's heartbeats, and deep within you can fathom its presence, but you cannot put your hands on it. At times the wandering heart is out on long hunts for contentment. The mind goes prowling on worldly and unworldly adventures. However, the adventurous mind and heart return to their abode, the soul. They cling to it like toddlers holding on to their mothers for want of support. And the soul is faithful to its host until the final call comes from the Creator.

At times when a human starts acting and thinking in a way heedless to the moral boundaries of the soul, the soul is burdened. But it has to be patient, as the Creator wills its fate and so tells the conscience, "Hey, wait. We need dialogue to decide what is best for this being. Remember, your host will not rest in peace. A body must be balanced physically, ethically, and spiritually to breathe freely."

Inside a human's body, the soul pricks, gnaws, and hammers away while the heart and mind desire to play on life's versatile strings.

At times the heart asks the soul, "There is danger when this thing called imagination in the humans has me on roller-coaster rides. Imagination pulls my strings in uncanny ways. What do I do when I am led down unwanted paths?"

"The soul needs constant nurturing to keep it alive physically and emotionally, but imagination, the key to creativity can open countless doors to infinity and eternity for humans. At such moments, the soul balances the waves on stormy and calm seas," replies the soul.

When a mind becomes confused about its host's rational thoughts, it reaches out to the soul, and the soul says in the voice of Blaise Pascal, "The heart has its reasons of which reason knows nothing."

The mind agrees, "I cannot unlock the deepest secret of the human heart. The Creator, like many of his mysteries, keeps it hidden even from other fellow beings." After a pause the mind says in a troubled voice, "I am in dilemma when this thing called "imagination" starts its unpredictable rides."

The Creator clears up his instruction regarding this wild ingredient He has given to the human brain. "Imagination is the source of the creative fountain in humans. The imagination has the freedom to travel from one corner of the world to the other and beyond. It can travel to the past, stay in the present, or go to the future. However, in the end, it returns to its abode—the soul. And then it's your job to shape it, remodel it, plus and minus it to suit the host, and have it ready to sail again. The imagination and the heart are like horses that need to be kept on reign."

And this unique quality given to humans, imagination, is having its adventures with two souls, Tareq and Daisy. Almost four weeks after their intense and delicious lovemaking, Daisy is suffering morning sickness. She has happily just missed her menstrual cycle. Tareq and Daisy imagine babies crawling around their home. At times they envision a little girl with round pink cheeks like Daisy's, and at times they dream that it will be a sweet tan boy like Tareq. Often they huddle close, softly talking away of the baby that seems to be on the way.

But do they know that a soul is already sharing their life? That the soul is already inside Daisy? The Creator has His own plans. He has already decided the sex of the baby. The parents will know when the time comes.

Part Four

Dancing Lights

five

Daisy is already on the lookout for names. She makes trips to bookshops to search for good books to help her choose the name of the coming baby. To Tareq she asks, "Darling, shall we give our baby a Bangladeshi name, or an American one? Maybe we can come up with a mix."

It is evening and both are relaxing after dinner in the family room where they have a huge sofa to stretch out on together. Daisy is thinking that choosing a flower's name or a bird's name for the child might be a good idea. Nature seems to be set apart from the human world of competition.

"I love everything in your land, sweetheart," Tareq says, and he hugs his wife who is huddling close to him. The softness of her body combined with the fragrance of her shampoo exudes a unique sense of closeness, something that exists just for him. Kissing her softly on her neck, he says, "Indeed, I would have an English first name, something that is similar to your name."

Their bodies are like two magnets, instantly attracted to one another. They can seldom resist the excitement their bodies evoke when close. As Tareq kisses Daisy, she feels her whole being gushing with sensations and turns her face upward, her lips eagerly inviting his. As they make love on the sofa, the TV screen flashes streaks of light on the heaving bodies in the dark room. Tareq had remembered to turn the lights off, and their clothes are strewn on the floor in the dark.

Afterward they lay still, holding each other. Exhausted but happy, Tareq remarks, "You know, people say the love of the heart must be strong before sex comes onto the scene. But I think they come together for a man and a woman truly matched. Can you feel the vibrations of my body for you? Why, I can hardly wait till I can take you again, and it seems to be so natural to our love."

But all he hears in response is Daisy's gentle breathing. She is fast asleep. He smiles as he plays with her curly hair. She seems to become tired easily these days.

As Tareq and Daisy debate the naming of their first child, those in the invisible world of the souls ask questions about names and other issues of the human world. In the Land of Illumination, all the souls share a name; they are all called "Dancing Light." The Creator's voice penetrates their beings, and He passes this name into their ears when they are created and sent to the Land of Illumination. They share this common name until they enter human bodies. After a baby is born, the soul exists with the name of its human host.

From the Land of Illumination, the souls named Dancing Light depart, but humans make a big fuss of naming the babies in which the souls reside. The names differ depending on whether the baby is a boy or a girl. Names differ in so many ways. Language, personal likes and dislikes, family traditions, and a many other things influence the naming of a child.

In the Land of Illumination, a soul back from her life in the human world quivers her nose and says, "Humans often ask each other, 'What's in a name?' Their well-known writer William Shakespeare has left this dialogue for the generations: 'A rose by any other name would smell as sweet.'"

She then adds, "I was named Beautiful, for my parents wanted to make my host feel good about my not-too-pleasing appearance. If naming is so important, is a girl named Sweetie truly sweet in nature? Or does a boy named Good Heart become a man of a generous heart?"

A wise genie who has come just in time offers an explanation, "There is no proof of the truth of a name's influence on a person. But men and women can fall in and out of love for the sake of a name. Numbers do not stir emotions as much as words do. Human beings are very much influenced by words. But they name the robots with numbers."

The souls that are waiting to enter the human world are in great apprehension of names they are going to be given on Earth.

six

Dancing Lights consider their lives in the Land of Illumination heavenly. For them it is their happy place. They know that in the human world life is tough.

Before descending to the human world, all souls have to take baths, cleansing themselves in preparation for the challenges that lie in wait for them. An ice-water bath is given to each to remind them that they will be doused with pain and sadness at times. After this they sit together around a bonfire made out of pure sandalwood branches. The intense heat alerts them to how it feels to be touched with fire. And at times, their voices float through air, crying, "Ouch, that ice water is cold!" or "Aw, that fire is scalding!"

They cannot help but scream out when they are given touches of ice and fire. Expression is essential to making humans feel good or bad. They need an outlet to voice anger, resentment, or joy.

One soul who had just been dipped in icy water complains, "Why must we go through these terrible experiences before we are with the humans? We have to go through them once we are there, anyway!"

An angel sitting nearby ready to take the next batch of souls to Earth replies, "The Creator loves his unique human creations. To synchronize the physical and the emotional beings, the souls are touched with fire, water, and ice. If you souls do not experience these feelings, you will not react appropriately when in your bodies. You might harm your hosts out of ignorance, and so you have to experience these feelings before you are sent down."

Another angel waiting speaks up and explains to a descending soul. "See these flowers, these butterflies? Feel the wind touching you with its sweetness? They fill your aesthetic senses so that when the human brain wants to respond to feelings and visions of love and beauty, you will not reject them. You see, the soul is lovingly created by the Creator as the very essence of the body that it enters. Harmony is essential to a good life. The greatest harmony that the Creator wants is that between the body and soul. There must be the ubiquitous presence of honesty and goodness, for these are the lights that show them the way to the Creator."

"What happens when someone falls short of this balance?" asks another soul that has just had its taste buds groomed with all the tastes that may come its way. This soul is preparing to enter the body of a male chef.

An angel sitting close to the parting souls gets up, for he feels the pull of gravity and the need to descend soon with the waiting souls. Before going downward, he says, "The tongue tastes bitter, sweet, sour, hot, and what not? The Creator is the most meticulous and knows that a human body relies for its nutrition on food. And so the stomach, tongue, hunger, and brain all must work together to bring forth the bounty of food that He provides for man. Even there is another puzzle; all humans are not fed or clothed equally. The fortunate and the less fortunate of these humans are chosen like a throw of the Creator's dice."

When a soul is sent to Earth, the other souls have a special song to accompany it on its journey. "Soul Melody," as the song is called, is a part of the souls' beings. Like the birds they sing sweet melodies, but the songs are spiritual songs that echo in the wind. It mingles with the birds' songs, with the rushing and roaring sound of the sea, with the swish of the wind, with the shrill of the storm, and every sound that comes from the unseen. Until the souls reach their hosts, they continue to hear this mystic song.

Life flow, flow.
Beat with the heart
and keep in the flow.
With the mind,
keep in the flow.
Call the Creator,
He be all in all...

After learning the song, one soul comes up with a perplexing question. She asks, "Some humans are said to be confused about the Creator's creations. They believe that everything happens under the law of science. How do we direct them to the existence of the Creator?"

The Creator reveals, "I appreciate the humans' quest for knowledge. I lead them on to discover the causes and effects of all that happens around them. They know about the movement of the celestial world, the underwater world, and of the life on Earth. And yet while they gather evidence, at times they come to dead ends. They find that the evidence they have found can change within the matter of a second. Baffled by the changes of established facts, they exclaim, 'Who is this mysterious force that riddles our visions and wisdom?' And here I sit and wonder: When will my creations see me as their Creator?"

The human world is like the Creator's playground, where human beings, like puppets, play out their roles in life. He waits for the day when they start playing life's games in the easy way, with honesty and truth. But he encourages humans to protest when they are wronged by their fellow beings. He has given humans their consciences to feel the right and wrong. And it is this question of right and wrong that keeps humans on their seats of judgment.

Part Five

Tareq and Daisy: North Carolina Chapter

seven

One fine day at summer's end, the Creator is making the entry of a soul known to its father and mother, for Tareq and Daisy were not certain of Daisy's pregnancy until the doctor confirmed it. It is on this day that they spread the good news to their friends. Tareq calls his mother, Momota, and tells her of her coming grandchild. The old lady, in Bangladesh is thrilled. She is going to be a "Dadi," meaning grandmother in Bangla, Tareq's mother tongue.

Enter, enter, invisible soul to the hearts of friends and family! Thunder seems to explode, mountains come crashing down, and seas go wild with the power of the new life being released to Earth. Each life is another unique creation of the Creator. But the humans wonder if sending life to Earth is like releasing puppets on strings for the Giver of Life. He is the one who controls the fates of his creations. The happy news is spread to almost everyone Tareq and Daisy know.

"You play with humans like a toddler absorbed with its childish whims and yet there is endless jubilations for life," souls of relatives and friends exclaim to each other as they welcome the news of the unborn baby.

Immediately they hear from the Creator, "I couldn't be more serious. With each life I release, a part of me goes, for I am with my souls all the time."

And so here is Daisy, the American woman chosen to give birth to this new soul. Daisy had not conceived after three years of marriage. Tareq and she had consulted the best doctors in North Carolina. Daisy had a hard time being on medication for pregnancy. Bed rest, medication, and other restrictions were tough uphill battles, as day after day she hoped for the miracle to happen, for her pregnancy test to show a positive reading.

Now that Daisy knows of her coming baby, she feels confident about the unborn child that is already a part of her life. Often she reflects on the motherhood that is coming to her.

"Mothers always seem to understand their children better than fathers," Daisy murmurs to herself, as she gently touches her belly, as if communicating to the new life inside her. She goes on. "Now that I am going to be a mother, I will understand more about the mother and child relationship. I will give my baby a life with unconditioned love, especially when it comes to romance."

Falling in love had been a sublime experience for Daisy. She has always been helpless where her heart is concerned. Her parents' lack of understanding when it came to Tareq's presence in her life really disappointed Daisy. However, she forgets the anxieties over her parents' absence in her life the day she is notified by her doctor that, finally, she is going to have her baby.

Daisy is ecstatic. The long wait is finally being rewarded, and it is a miracle the Creator has blessed her with. There is so much to do in regard to her health care now. She has to add nutrition to her diet to make sure that the baby will be strong. Excited like many pregnant women, Daisy is running to grocery stores and busy preparing healthful meals. Tareq often cooks fish in the Bangladeshi style for her, for she likes the spicy flavor of the dishes.

At three months of pregnancy, Daisy's belly is showing the signs of new life. There is a blessed look on Daisy's face, for her swollen belly brings her light and hope. Becoming a mother is a source of joy, the fulfillment of a biological hunger.

On the doctor's recommendation, Daisy and Tareq undergo a sex test of the coming baby. They are full of joy when it is pronounced the girl that they have wanted all along. They try to visualize a little girl with the blended features of American and Bangladeshi parentage.

"Hi, sweetie, we are going to name you Lotus Khan." Both of them talk to the baby growing inside the womb.

Often at night Tareq puts his hands on his wife's belly, kisses it, and says, "Thank you, Creator, for blessing us with a child." He kisses Daisy long and hard and says, "Thanks, love, for carrying our child."

When Daisy fell in love with this stranger, it was for his loving nature. He is strong and determined, yet with a heart as soft as butter. Daisy always laughs when Tareq objects to being compared with butter. She says, "Jaan, your heart is butter; you melt away with love for anyone who needs you. I'm glad I found you before any other woman."

Tareq has taught her to call him *Jaan*, meaning "heart".

eight

The world around Daisy is going on with excitement, for the coming baby and the days' normal routines are in upheaval. But she has to balance it all with peaceful sunsets and some restless nights that seem to be a part of pregnancy. As the pregnancy marches ahead, she is finding it difficult to rise early for her job. Her work as a consultant keeps her busy, but she has signed up for shorter hours since becoming pregnant. All her dreams revolve around the unborn child growing in her womb. The way ahead is full of dazzling lights. She is immensely happy.

Daisy is not sure how she is linked to the spiritual world through her child, but she feels content, a blessing inside her heart. It is all so because the Creator has sent a soul called Dancing Light to the fetus that is to be called Lotus Khan. Now Daisy carries two souls inside her—her own and the new one sent to her baby.

At times she seems to hear someone whispering to her, "Now your priority is to take care of yourself and the baby. Eat well, think of all the good things, and be happy. Your emotions affect your baby's health and growth." Daisy is not aware, but it is her own soul talking to her from time to time.

Daisy is conscious of the great physical changes within her body and is awed. At times she wishes that she could penetrate the world of creation where the Creator goes on playing with the lives he sends down. Her swollen belly makes her wobble like a penguin these days. Her breasts are becoming heavier as they get ready to supply the new baby with mother's milk. Every day she is going on the Internet to learn about motherhood. Tareq and she go to the parenting center to discuss the delivery and how to be better parents. Daisy's soul hears a special message from the Creator, for Daisy constantly asks for His help.

The Creator sends a revelation to Daisy's soul, saying, "I am transmitting information about how to keep Daisy healthy so that you can do a better job of getting her heart, mind, and the conscious being into harmony. I want my creations to live in peace and health."

Dancing Light, Lotus's soul, knows that the little girl about to come out into the world is supposed to have her own personality. But in the womb, while the little unborn child's heart goes on beating, Daisy is constantly praying to the Creator to bless her child with a worthy life. Daisy seems to want to put into the unborn child some part of her own personality. So Daisy's soul tells Dancing Light, "Daisy, like many other mothers of her kind, is afraid of change, and so would like to have a child that she can easily understand, and like many mothers, she wishes her child to be like herself."

Dancing Light hears the Creator's voice filtering into her. "This is a frequent tendency among parents; they want their children to be like them. You have to keep sending the mother's whims to the unborn just to keep the mother and child in harmony. But once in the world, you will enlighten the little girl with her own thoughts and put her own values into her consciousness. She will grow with her own personality and will be nourished by the love and good wishes of her mother. Every child inherits some personality traits from the parents and the ancestors."

Already worried about the challenges of guiding Lotus, Dancing Light wonders if the little girl will abide by her mother's wishes once she is aware that she has a mind of her own. She takes the dreams of the mother and transmits them to the child in the womb. Dancing Light has been given the gift to time travel, and so she can see how the child will do after coming into the world. Soon, Dancing Light knows that Lotus's heart and mind will work in mysterious ways, ways that her mother will not understand. However, beyond a certain time frame, Dancing Light cannot see the future, for the Creator allows only as much time travel as He thinks best for Lotus.

Dancing Light, upon asking questions regarding developing Lotus's personality, hears the Creator say, "The blending of others' personality traits to create a completely new child is what makes each human unique. Parents are to remember that the children are blessings from the Creator. The parents do not own their children—life does. Like the parents themselves, they live life in transition. Parents have to let go and allow their children to grow in their own ways."

But Dancing Light honors Daisy's wishes. After all, carrying a child in the womb for nine months is not easy for a mother. So to let her have peace, and with the Creator's consent, Dancing Light puts some of Daisy's wishes into Lotus.

However, Daisy's soul has to be very diplomatic while she honors her host's thoughts and emotions. She has to keep track of Dancing Light's whims and keep her host content. Together, they are aware that it is teamwork that is important while Lotus is still inside the womb.

Dancing Light is having her first experiences of a mother's love for her child. Daisy's heart, mind, and soul are overflowing with love for the new life. Daisy's prayers for a healthy child with goodness radiating all around and through is constantly being transmitted to Dancing Light.

Daisy's soul advises Dancing Light to accept the mother's wishes and dreams for the child before she enters the big, big world. A mother never harbors evil thoughts to pass onto her child. In other words, it is like planting the seed of love in Dancing Light, so that with this strength she will sail through life with all its ups and downs. And thus Dancing Light takes love to work with its endlessness virtues. In her time travels, she has seen a tough life ahead for Lotus.

While Dancing Light transmits the mother's wishes to Lotus, she keeps some of them on hold. Like a blooming flower, the moral being of Lotus will be opened by Dancing Light the moment she is born. The righteous ways of the Creator will be filtered into her heart and mind along with her other physical and mental developments. Lotus will have her personality developed in different stages, and Dancing Light will wake her to a meaningful life.

The Creator is blessing Lotus with senses, so she can hear His message to her: "Behold your Creator within you, outside you, and beyond. Every moment you breathe is through him. No one knows this better than the souls that keep you while you are on Earth!"

An expecting mother, Daisy has a special place among other women. She is touched by how her colleagues in the consultancy office are always considerate of her motherhood. She goes to her boss one day, feeling rather too worn out to work, and asks for an early maternity leave. The boss, Kumiko Yushonari, a Japanese American, smilingly says, "Ah Daisy, you are not eating enough. You know in our country we always say the pregnant mother has to eat for two."

Beautiful with black glossy hair, Kumiko speaks with a foreign accent when speaking English. Daisy cannot but smile at her boss as she says the "two" with a soft "thu." She cannot pronounce the hard consonants of some words English words. But she is a good boss, kind and efficient. Daisy feels happy as she is granted her maternity leave, knowing that her job will be waiting for her when she returns after her baby is born.

A mother's dreams for her child are like flowers on the wheels of eternity. With the first steps into pregnancy, Daisy wonders how she will dress her baby girl before taking her to daycare on her way to the office. Will she use pink ribbons or purple more often? Will she buy dresses with frills or will she be practical and settle for T-shirts?

nine

These days Daisy spends much of her time on Google, intensely browsing for information on pregnancy and childcare. It seems as though she is back in school, a school for motherhood. This becomes more real as Tareq suggests they join the Mother's Club nearby and take regular lessons until the child is born.

"Lovey-Dovey" is what Tareq calls her when he is in a pampering mood. He holds his hands on her growing belly and says, "Hey, kid in the womb, remember that your Mom and I both are bringing you into the world because we want a fruit of our love."

Tareq kisses Daisy's swelling belly and lets her lie down with her head on his lap. He runs his fingers gently through her golden curls and says, "Suppose we have a baby with your blue eyes and my black hair and then a mixture of your white and my brown skin. Why, she would grow into a real beauty!"

"Ah, Daddy Tareq." Daisy gives him a quick kiss on his chin dimple beneath his wide and generous mouth and says, "So you are very, very happy we are going to have a baby girl?"

He kisses her enlarged breasts over the blouse, smiles naughtily, and says, "Aha, Dad's sucking of these beautiful breasts will soon be replaced by the fruit of our love."

"Hey, you jealous brute!" Daisy gives give him a playful smack on the back and then holds his head down on her bosom. They sit for long hours just like that, the warmth of their bodies seeping into each other.

At home they share quiet hours of just being together. Daisy often sits with Tareq in their kitchen as he prepares the dinner. Tareq is very affectionate and gentle, and it is these traits that Daisy fell for while they were earning master's degrees at North Carolina State University. She has her degree in economics, and he has his in electrical engineering.

Thinking of their past campus days and classes, she wonders how a stranger from so far away could win her heart. For her his looks, ethnicity, and culture served no significant impediment to getting to know him better. Daisy still recalls how shyly Tareq had kissed her on their third date.

Fond memories come to Daisy of that day, when she had so happily known her love was reciprocated.

"I have never kissed a woman before in my life, you know," he had said when he took her in his arms. At first he was a bit awkward, but Daisy had told him to hold her tightly. And when he did, it was practically to enmesh her body with his. Pausing between long kisses, she had said, "If you can't hold me tightly enough, I will be gone."

"Ah, no, lady," he had said. "I cannot let you go."

He held on to her tightly, as if scared of her threat, and he deeply inhaled the scent of her golden hair. Her perfume had filled his nose even before he took her in his arms, and with her body crumpled into his embrace he felt dizzy. Daisy was mesmerized by him. She could smell the manly odor emanating from his body, and she snuggled her head on his chest while her arms circled him. Both clung to each other.

As they kissed endlessly, Daisy heard him murmur under his breath, "How can I tell you how much I want you?"

Daisy felt his hands dig into her back. No, he wanted her in a way other than just this holding of bodies. He forgot the barrier of his culture, his family values. She was supposed to keep herself a virgin until they took their wedding vows. He was supposed to be the keeper of the sacredness of their love until the special night. But that night, mutual consent and surrender to a deeper desire were written in their eyes as they held on to their passing warmth.

They were in Daisy's place when they had both surrendered to that surge of love. It was a glorious night for both of them. They just could not have enough of each other, as their bodies entwined, heaved, and rocked with passion. He had loved her, endlessly accepting her as she was, calling her his "American Witch."

"What magic spell did you cast on me, Jaan?" he had asked again and again as their lovemaking found them relentless. In his heart he knew that it was the graciousness, the goodness in Daisy that enchanted him. He was helplessly in love and their lust seemed to have no end.

Daisy too had accepted the foreigner as he was, seeing his good heart beyond the boundaries of land and sea. As they lay in each other's arms until the morning, she thought that love had no definition at all, no address either. She just couldn't find the right words to tell Tareq how happy she was.

As if to wake her from her reverie, Daisy's cell phone vibrates with a chime, announcing an incoming message. After checking the message, an update of the day's weather, Daisy settles back to a book she is reading about taking care of newborn baby girls. She is planning the next trip to the library to get books on dressing her daughter.

ten

Lotus is twenty weeks old in her mother's womb. She is developed to a stage where she can follow some of her mother's feelings. Unknown to Daisy, with the Creator's added strength; she can communicate to the outside world through Dancing Light, her soul. At times Lotus feels a sudden spell of anxiety pass through her body as he follows her mother. Lotus is eavesdropping while Daisy talks with an aunt who is visiting her grandmother in Bangladesh. The aunt says she was hoping for a grandson who would carry the family name. In Bangladesh the male child is taken to be very special. Lotus is upset thinking that she is not welcome in the family.

Daisy's soul convinces Lotus that having her parents happy is what really matters. Daisy is already planning a room in her house, all in pink with pictures of angels and Hello Kitty posters. The baby cot, the curtains, and chest of drawers are all to be in pink. And Daisy wants curtains with white frills too. She wants to make the room look girly but is apprehensive, wondering if the constant reminders to the girl of her sex might take away the strength she will need to compete in society alongside men. She calls her friend Linda, a mother of three brilliant daughters, and asks, "Linda, your daughters are doing great in school and extracurricular activities. Do you think giving only girlish things to my coming baby girl will affect her development?"

Linda chuckles and says, "Parenting is no easy job, Daisy. You never know what lies under the oceans. By all means make yourself happy. Give her all the pink touches, but make sure to let her know that as a girl or woman, she is always equal to the opposite sex."

Dancing Light whispers to Lotus, "See how happy your mother is to have you! People in Bangladesh still think boys are family torchbearers, but wait until you grow up, get educated, and show them all what women can really do."

Dancing Light watches silently as Daisy and Tareq go to an office to complete paperwork for the coming child. They are getting insurance for Lotus's health care and are already naming her the nominee of their bank accounts when she reaches the age of eighteen.

Daisy's mother has started visiting her daughter. Time, the best healer has softened her heart and she has given her house in Ashville to Daisy. But Daisy was told not to speak of this gift with her father, for he is still mad about Tareq. Daisy implored Tareq to go through the formalities and make arrangements, enabling their coming child to inherit the property at the age of twenty.

While the parents work for the future of their coming baby, Lotus floats in the sticky liquid of her mother's womb, drinking and eating all that is coming through the umbilical cord. Dancing Light puts thoughts of anticipations into Lotus, filling her with the light of love and care her parents are waiting to give her. She tells the unborn baby that once in Daisy's lap, Lotus will feel safe and adored.

When Lotus feels impatient and starts kicking her feet, hurting her mom, Daisy gently touches the bulging spots in her belly and says, "Kiddo, wait. You are better off inside me, you know. The world out here is not so easy!"

※

With time Lotus forms strings of attachment to both parents, she feels happy and sad for them. Lotus's budding soul feels tremors of unhappiness passing like a feathery thread when one night Daddy wants to make love to Mommy, and she does not want it.

"My love, can I have those wonderful cherries?" says Daddy, enfolding his arms around Daisy's soft and supple body. He starts nuzzling her neck, his hands moving all over the body he loves so much.

Daisy puts a hand on his tussled hair and says gently, "Darling, I am feeling so exhausted. Can you wait until morning? I'll feel refreshed after the night's sleep!"

Lotus's young soul can feel the tiredness of her mother's pregnancy, and she can feel the weakness that seems to cloud Mommy's mind too. Strange it may be, but Lotus feels sad for Daddy too, for he seems unhappy. Her soul seems to share ties with Daddy's thought, even as she remains in Daisy's womb. Lotus feels pangs of love for her father. And yet she is feeling the weight of a sad Mommy on her soul. She hears Mommy whisper to the pillow as tears cling to her eyes,

"Why can't men understand how different the body feels when one is pregnant? He loves me, but at times seems to be like a child with his demands. Men, they become crazy when they want sex."

As Dancing Light and Daisy's soul tug the chord for the Creator's assistance in this confusion between husband and wife, Dancing Light becomes aware of someone's presence in the room as Tareq drifts off to sleep. Dancing Light sees an angel hovering over the couple. As the angel touches Daisy and Tareq, they feel peace fill their hearts.

Tareq kisses his wife full on the mouth and says, "Sorry, sweetheart, I know you are exhausted."

The faint bluish light from the angel fills the room, and Dancing Light whispers, "Is there someone here helping these confused adults?"

A voice echoes back, "Did you not seek help from the Creator because your parents were momentarily unhappy? I am an angel sent down by the Creator to help these two good souls sail through this trying period of life. From now on, I will be with Daisy and watch over her while the pregnancy lasts."

Dancing Light feels relief flood over her. The Creator is generous indeed when he sees good intentions in his beings. Lotus, now twenty-eight weeks old in her mom's womb, seems to be opening like a flower. Gradually Daisy's belly becomes more and more swollen. As Lotus becomes larger, she can feel Mommy's fatigue in carrying her. Yet she can also feel the joy in her heart.

Lotus hears her mother talking to her friend over the mobile phone, saying, "I can hardly wait until this baby is born. Is there any way of taking it out sooner? I can hardly sit, sleep, or walk."

The ripple of anticipation for the coming world gives a boost to Lotus. She wants to grow larger at a faster rate so that she can enter the world sooner. It seems to Lotus that the world outside is waiting for her. She has to get out of this slushy fluid in which Mommy is nurturing her. Lotus feels impatient. "Why do I have to wait so long?" Lotus asks Daisy's soul almost every day.

Daisy's soul talks to Dancing Light. "This baby is so impatient, even in the womb! What will she do once out? Why, Lotus is already well versed in channel surfing and even understands the computer keyboard. These digital kids are born gadget oriented."

Daisy's soul scoffs at Dancing Light as the new soul tries to accommodate Lotus's advanced learning skills.

In other ways, too, Lotus is showing life: pulsating, kicking, and boxing whenever she is not in tune with her life in the womb. Who wants to be fed with what Mommy considers healthy food? Spinach, chicken broth, fruits, and vegetables make her kick really hard. Dancing Light is working hard to slow down Lotus as she kicks and clenches her fists and hits the walls of Daisy's womb. But her mother cannot hear her shouting, "Let me out! Let me out!"

Lotus has little idea that the Creator will not allow her to be born before the destined time. But Dancing Light is doing what she has been sent to do–guide Lotus in the right way.

When Daisy feels the little fists and feet inside her womb, she puts her hands on her protruding belly and says, "Oh my child, I love you and cannot wait for you to come out to sit in my lap, but have patience for your own good."

Dancing Light feels vexed. The mother and child are impatient, and yet the Creator has planned the exact day, minute, and second for Lotus to be out. Dancing Light confides to Daisy's soul, "I am relaxed while in the womb. The day Lotus leaves, my trepidations will begin. How I will have to be with Lotus with all her laughter and tears. I hope she is a bit late in leaving. Even if it is only a week, it will still give me a bit more time."

"Don't worry, I can see Daisy being a good mother to Lotus and guiding her. But in my time travel, I see a challenging road ahead in the world. The strangest thing is that I can't see Tareq nearby. I wonder what the Creator has written in the little girl's fate. Why do I see a vision of such short travel with her father on her life's journey?"

eleven

Daisy is marking off the weeks on the calendar: twenty-eight weeks, thirty weeks, thirty-two weeks, and so on. Lotus can feel the echoes of Mommy's impatience and patience—impatient to see the baby she is growing inside her and patient because she knows a full nine months is best for little Lotus. Daisy talks to Lotus while she gently rotates her hands over her swollen belly.

"Hey, we go to the doctor tomorrow," she says as she packs a bag for the hospital visit.

Lotus gives off happy kicks and moves her tiny fists so that they make tiny mounds against her mother's skin, as if acknowledging her mother's words. Lotus is already sending vibes about her likes and dislikes to her mother. Avocado is in Daisy's daily breakfast menu and so is plain yogurt. Lotus finds these things disgusting. Dancing Light sends a message to Daisy's soul that her baby does not like those foods, but the mother is bent on having these two items on her daily menu.

And so Dancing Light, already tuned in to indulge Lotus at times, whispers to her, giving her a playful nudge. "Hey, Lotus, move a lot when Mom eats avocado and yogurt, and that will make her throw up. That should discourage her from eating them. Do that every time she eats those foods."

"Good advice. That is a good way to protest about anything I don't like." Lotus exclaims to Dancing Light.

She listens to music that Daisy often puts on the audio set. It's John Denver's "Country Roads." Lotus does not like it. Dancing

Light is there to help her develop her aesthetic senses. She asks Daisy's soul to tell her host to play some Greek music. Daisy's soul has her host listen to a song by Meat Loaf, "I'd Do Anything for Love (But I Won't Do That)," as well as some Bangla songs. Lotus likes Bangla songs. She inherited some of her father's tastes in music.

Lotus likes these songs better. She lies still in her liquid while her ears strain to hear the music. The blood travelling through her mom's body at times makes a hissing sound that makes it difficult for Lotus to connect to her mom. But listening to music makes Daisy feels calm, lowering her blood pressure, and Lotus can hear the music better.

"Thanks," Dancing Light says to Daisy's soul. "See how Lotus is gurgling with happiness? She likes the flow of these new tunes, and next time you must guide Daisy to buy some Greek music. I know Lotus will like that."

With Dancing Light transmitting the unborn child's contentedness and discontentedness to Daisy through her soul, Lotus is nurtured with the best of physical and mental support. That is the Creator's magic, bonding the souls of the mother and the child through food and thought even before the mother sees her baby's face.

Lotus wants things to be really quiet at night. Nearing the day of her delivery, she can feel the difference of day and night more vividly, even from the depth of the womb. Her senses are now fully developed. But Mom has recently started staying awake, clicking away on her laptop. Daisy often lies on the bed with her back propped up with pillows and the laptop on the bedside table. The bedside table, pulled nearer, is convenient for her huge belly that seems to be running ahead of her into everything, and she cannot sit for long. Lotus can hear her mother's fingers clicking away on the keyboard.

Lotus hates the chatting sessions Daisy holds with her friends on Facebook. In the status section, she shares the pains and pleasures of pregnancy. And when Daisy goes on Skype, Lotus can feel the vibrations of the dialogue travelling on sound waves right through her tender ears. Daisy talks for long hours to some of her friends in other states. When she is engaged on Facetime on the iPhone, Lotus can see the people Daisy talks to.

"Hey, Daisy, how is the baby?" This is the question most often asked as Daisy chats online.

Lotus is curious to hear or read when Daisy is busy with social networking. She is already the curious cat. The Creator added special reading abilities to Dancing Light so that Lotus can read along with Daisy. The Creator has done His updating of the souls with special abilities to connect with other souls on the Internet. Dancing Light has lively chatting sessions with other souls when Daisy is online.

But Dancing Light is alarmed when the unborn child's body reacts to radiation passed from the electric gadgets used by Daisy. She passes the message to Daisy's soul, who replies, "Technology really traps these people. They don't even think twice about the radiation hazards on their children. I better ask the soul of Daisy's friend Nancy, a doctor, to alert the expecting mother of the risks of electronics."

Daisy's soul is happy to hear Nancy talking to Daisy over the phone, telling her, "Daisy, take barefoot walks in the garden every morning to fight the effects of the electromagnetic radiation. It helps a lot to have the solid earth beneath your feet, and the fresh air is good. Use microwaves as little as possible. That excess heating of the food changes its DNA, and so what is your child inside the womb eating? It's almost as good as plastic!"

Lotus has learned the tricks of having her way from the womb. Whenever her mother has late nights, Lotus starts kicking until Daisy retires. Lotus feels happy when her mother spends time bonding with nature and sits under the large oak tree in the nearby park. She is very still, allowing her mother to sit in peace, and it is here that they are best able to talk.

"Hey, baby, look! The trees are so beautiful this summer. Can you hear the birds' songs? I love my North Carolina, my home, and I want you to grow up in this nature's abundance. As soon as I can, I'll take you to the Blue Ridge Mountains." And, as usual, Daisy moves her hands over the big belly.

People passing by in the park often smile knowingly at the expecting mother. They can see the dreams of happiness written in Daisy's eyes.

At times, Daisy hums her favorite songs and taps on her belly, as if asking the baby to listen. Thus Daisy tries to connect to Lotus, being advised by her doctor to communicate with the life in her womb. It's supposed to be healing to the stress of pregnancy.

"Lotus, see those sweet peas, daffodils, roses, and blue weeds? Aren't they beautiful? And that heavenly fragrance of roses, do you sense it?"

As Daisy talks, Lotus sends a soft tremor of movement, as if to tell her mom that she is listening to her. If encouraged by the trembling she feels, Daisy goes on talking and talking to the unborn child, sometimes even telling her about things that have made her sad or happy. But Daisy cannot help but wonder how it will be to raise a child in this competitive world.

twelve

Dancing Light is busy learning life lessons from Daisy's soul during the evenings these days, usually when Daisy is just sitting with Tareq, enjoying a movie or ice cream. Lotus is being passed personality traits from her ancestors, some as old as five generations back. The humans call this genetics. This seems to be the Creator's way of keeping the present indebted to the past. Humans learn lessons from successes and failures of the past.

It is a daunting task, for at times Daisy's soul would direct Dancing Light into time travel to find an ancestor from decades back. Dancing Light must meet the spirits of those ancestors and pass some of his or her looks and personality into Lotus. Daisy's soul is gentle as she explains to Dancing Light the reasons behind this order of the Creator.

"You see, it's our job to pass blood connections to the new generations. The Creator encourages the passing of good traits and discourages us from transmitting bad traits to the newborns, but at times the heart and the mind do not remember the messages of the ancestors."

Daisy's soul is aware that there are physically and mentally ill people Dancing Light will meet, and to prepare her for them, she goes on to say, "But at times, the Creator himself sends in physically or mentally challenged humans. It is a way of showing the comparison of blessings. Wealth too is not blessed equally. This is to make people appreciate what they have, to help them see the less fortunate ones. It is His way of reminding them that, up there, He is the one who gives life as he wishes."

"But humans who steal, kill, deceive, and lie, why do they commit these crimes? Aren't the good traits passed to them?" asks Dancing Light.

Daisy's soul replies, "This is the tough game we play with our intelligence that allows us to choose."

Just then Daisy's soul and Dancing Light become aware of an angel in the room. They are perfectly still as they listen to the angel passing on a divine message. The angel says, "Dancing Light, ask for the Creator's help and listen when messages are sent to you when you face confusions. Humans have been given two ears and one tongue so they are able to listen more and talk less. You can learn a lot through keeping careful track of all the revelations given unto you. The Creator does not want humans to live in ignorance, and the souls who will be guiding them must gain wisdom about life."

Dancing Light trembles with the enormity of helping her host grow, and so Lotus gives a big lurch. This makes Daisy come out with a loud *Ouch!* Her belly feels like a bursting grape.

Daisy and Tareq are sitting watching television when Daisy comes out with her exclamation. Tareq's hand immediately comes down on her belly, and quietly they feel the movement of their child. The silence is a profound silence. They move closer, and Tareq takes Daisy into the folds of his arms and holds her tightly.

Growing bigger and bigger seems to be the game of the day for Daisy. One morning, on a sudden impulse, Daisy runs to Tareq and taking his right hand places it on Lotus moving in her womb.

"Honey, feel the baby kicking inside. I'll soon be too heavy and will not be able move around much. We still have three weeks to go before the baby comes. I am just dying to see the crashing waves of the sea. Let's take a trip to Wilmington Beach. My heart is craving the sight of the plundering sea waves."

When he puts his right hand over his wife's big belly, Tareq feels the baby moving in Daisy's womb. It is as if the unborn child too is urging him to take her mommy to the seaside.

"Let's go, let's go! Make Daddy's soul agree," Lotus shouts to Daisy's soul.

Dancing Light's heart dances. *Oh it will be fun to visit the sea! We did not have this fun in the Land of Illumination!*

Tareq is free on the coming weekend, and so he decides to take Daisy to Wilmington Beach. It isn't too far from their place.

He kisses his wife lightly on her lips and says, "Okay, sweetheart, since you feel like going to the beach, let's go this weekend. Let me know if you need help with the packing. But keep your doctor's phone numbers at hand in case of an emergency. I don't know whether we are taking a risk or not. I shall have to drive very slowly and gently, right?" He kisses her soft hair that always seems to smell of herbs and flowers.

Daisy kisses him back, giving him a hug. "Tareq, do you know how special you are? You are the most generous soul and the most caring man I have ever met."

"My, my!" Tareq laughs. "You have figured out this Bangladeshi guy *after* marrying him? I had little idea that I would end up marrying an American woman when I immigrated here. You are the best thing to ever happen to me."

Tareq puts his arms fondly around his sweet, smiling wife. He reflects on the sea that they are soon to visit and thinks that his wife's whole being is as vast and wonderful as the waiting mass of water.

thirteen

On the morning of their trip to Wilmington Beach, Daisy is full of anticipation. She is not at all daunted by the expected pains of delivering her child. Rather she calls out to Tareq, who is busy packing some sandwiches and fruits to eat on the way. "We could have at least four children. I like big families, okay, darling?" Daisy says as she packs clothes. On an impulse she adds, "You know I am going to allow my children to grow up with lots of freedom." Daisy's cheerful mood has her dreaming of a house full of children and good days for the future.

Listening to Daisy, Dancing Light is a bit confused over some details of this conversation, and she asks Daisy's soul, "Isn't it the Creator's choice to send the children? How can Daisy and Tareq plan on the number of children they will have?"

Smiling wisely, Daisy's soul says, "Oh these human beings have found ways to control their baby production. But don't think it always works!"

"The humans are clever. Why do their systems fail?" asks Dancing Light.

Daisy's soul shakes her head, as if Dancing Light is too innocent to understand such things. "At times the Creator does not give babies, even when humans are not using birth control. And when He wants, He can even make a big hole in the rubber thing the males use to stop the sperm from oozing out to fertilize the female eggs, and the result is the coming of a new life because the Creator wills it. The women who take birth control pills are made to forget the pills, and so the Creator again has his will."

While Dancing Light and Daisy's soul talk, a spirit passing by peeks in and says, "Remember, even after all the birth control systems and the medical science that has been developed to help women conceive, still it is the Creator's will to decide if a soul is to survive or not. Many babies die during delivery."

Seeing the spirit, Daisy's soul feels uneasy. Spirits are related to dead people, and that makes her wonder why they are hovering around. Some ominous messages seem to come to her. However, Dancing Light, humbled by how the Creator works, remarks, "Creating life and taking it away…. This is where the Creator is the Almighty."

"My, little one, you do learn fast!" says the spirit as she glides on, called by the Creator to go elsewhere.

The invisible souls have their talks while Daisy and Tareq prepare for the trip to the beach. In North Carolina, summer comes with rain, heat, and the residents are used to the full blast of the season. The raincoats and umbrellas are a part of the daily gear needed to go out. Thunder, lightning, and rain can start out of nowhere, even on a sunny day.

Daisy has an uncanny feeling about the trip, though her heart is calling out to the sea. She asks Tareq, "Have you checked the weather?"

Tareq, loading their car with water and food, replies, "Oh, the usual, rain and scattered thunderstorms mostly at night. Nothing to worry about."

But as Daisy and Tareq start on their way, they are feeling uneasy about the clouds gathering in the sky. Daisy's soul remembers the appearance of the spirit, and it gives her an eerie feeling.

"The rain seems to be coming really heavily now. See those ominous dark clouds?" Daisy remarks as they hit the highway.

Tareq, in the driver's seat, takes a brief look at his wife's worried face and says, "Relax, darling, I will drive carefully."

Dancing Light finds a connection to Daisy's soul and the two feel very uneasy. It's as if the day holds a warning of coming doom. Though Dancing Light has been very excited about the trip to Wilmington Beach, now that the moment is here she does not feel like going. She is aware that her host, Lotus, being the innocent baby she is, just sleeps and eats heartily through the worry. She seems to know that life on Earth is not easy, and she needs to suck in all the strength she can from Mommy. Dancing Light and Daisy's soul stare ahead. But they feel as if they are suspended on a scale that is swinging to and fro.

Tareq is driving his navy blue Toyota RAV4 slowly, for he does not want Daisy tensed by the speed. He is driving in the slow lane, sometimes whistling tunes that Daisy likes. On the radio they hear the song, "Summer Wine" with the lyrics, "Strawberries, cherries and an angel's kiss in spring...." This is Daisy's favorite song, and it momentarily lifts her anxiety as she taps her fingers on the dashboard with the beat of the music.

Her eyes are caught on Tareq's masculine hands, and then she takes a long look at her own chipped nails. Pedicures and manicures have been neglected with the weight of the pregnancy.

Just then, with a burst of thunder and streak of lightning, the rain starts relentlessly, large drops pattering against the windshield. Daisy and Tareq are midway to Wilmington Beach. They had hoped that rain would not catch them before reaching their destination. But soon the rain is so heavy that Tareq can hardly see even five or six feet ahead of them.

The pouring rain, the sight of water, makes Daisy feel like walking into the crashing waves of the waiting sea right there and then. But if it rains, that means staying in the hotel room. She wants so badly to sit on the sandy beach. However, she does not want to catch a cold in this late stage of pregnancy either. But this deep urge to see the sea is like a mad force driving her to take risks only a few weeks prior to her delivery.

Daisy remembers reading in a book that, "The pregnant mother has cravings and wants of the heart that gnaw until they are satisfied."

The car radio is playing sweet songs, and she hears Tareq saying, as if reading her thoughts, "You know even if it rains, you can go to the beach and stay on the sand. I will hold an umbrella over you. At least your heart will be glad to hear the hushing and rushing sound of the waves."

Tareq says this as he takes his eyes momentarily from the road. He could always read Daisy's thoughts like an open book. Daisy puts her right hand on the bulge of her belly where the baby is kicking. The baby, too, seems to be impatient to get a touch of the cool seawater.

Daisy laughs as she says, "Oh, well. You can read my thoughts, but what do you think Lotus is trying to say with all the kicks she is sending over?"

Dancing Light and Daisy's soul are sitting quietly near each other, both feeling fears tingling inside their beings, wondering what hidden events are coming to them. Why are they feeling these eerie feelings? The Creator has given them the ability to time travel, but queerly they can't at the moment. Some unseen force seems to be holding them back. Dancing Light and Daisy's soul brace themselves and pray for the Creator to help. As if the charging embodiment of their fears, they glimpse a red convertible coming from the opposite side of the highway. Suddenly Tareq seems to lose control of his car and heads straight toward the other car, or is the other car heading toward them? There is a blur. Next there is a loud crash. Daisy and Tareq both hear the other scream. And then there is complete silence.

As Daisy screams and her body goes limp after the terrible shock of the crash, Dancing Light has a vision of an angel lifting Daisy from the crashing car and holding her raised high as the cars meet in a head-on collision. In that moment she remembers that the Creator has assigned an angel for the new soul. Just for an instant, the angel holds Daisy and Lotus above the twisting metal and burning rubber, before gently placing them back in the car, safe from the shattered glass. Dancing Light can hear Daisy breathing with difficulty as she looks at Tareq. Only the Creator hears her scream as she looks at the blood-drenched, lifeless body, her voice so deep with anguish that no sound comes out.

Dancing Light and Daisy's soul reach out to each other. At least they are saved. Dancing Light feels grateful to the angel for keeping Lotus safe in her mother's womb. She stares at the angel as it, like a feather, drifts upward and vanishes.

Daisy's soul is alert to the unborn child and says to Dancing Light, "Give more life enhancing strength to Lotus. She got a bad jolt and needs life support. Pray for the Creator's help. Be ready. She may have to be taken out into the world today. I'll be busy taking care of the mother."

They look very sadly at the still body of Tareq, bathed with gushing blood, and are just in time to see Tareq's soul floating gently away, far away. They know the departing soul will return to the Land of Illumination with new stories for the souls, telling them how Tareq had migrated in hope of a long and good life in a faraway land, but that it was here that death awaited him.

Baffling are the ways of the Creator. Police arrive at the scene of the accident, and an ambulance carries Daisy to the hospital. Lotus is gasping for breath in the womb of her badly injured mother. The doctors and nurses get ready to do an immediate Caesarean section and get the baby out. They received Daisy with her water broken and the heartbeat of the baby growing weaker.

Inside Daisy's body, her soul and Dancing Light are having a hard time keeping the mother and the baby steady. Daisy's soul tells Dancing Light, "Hold on tight, the doctors are opening Daisy's womb to remove Lotus. The baby is almost blue."

And then Dancing Light can feel the strange hands as Lotus is gently taken out by the gloved hands of a female physician. The doctor takes out Lotus, and Dancing Light hears a soft, *Ouch!* It's Daisy's soul snorting as the doctor snips off the umbilical cord that tied the baby to the mother for so long.

Now it's Dancing Light who almost shouts as something hits her. "Ouch, what was that?"

Why is the doctor holding Lotus upside down and smacking her on the backside? She can hear the doctor murmuring softly, "Come on, baby, cry and start breathing properly. You can't give up now!"

Dancing Light is not ready for the final, hard smack the doctor gives the baby on the back, but it startles Lotus into crying, "*Wa...wa...wa...!*" Dancing Light hears her host whimpering.

Nurses take Lotus and clean up the blood and birth fluids that cover her body. They wrap her with soft white towels and put her in an incubator. Dancing Light hears the doctor saying that the baby will need days of intensive care, for she is very weak from the trauma of the accident.

Dancing Light is aware of an angel in the room. The angel says, "The Creator wills this life to enter the world despite the near-death experience. Keep praying for His help and *bon voyage* with your host in life! I was with her while she was in the womb, but now you will have other angels, genies, and her father's spirit coming to your aid when you call for the Creator's help."

Dancing Light would like to have the angel by her side a little longer, but she sees the angel rise slowly upward and disappear.

fourteen

As Daisy regains her senses, she can hear the beeps of machines around her and smell the disinfectants. "Where am I?" she says weakly. In a sudden flash, she remembers being on the road with Tareq. And now she mumbles softly, "Tareq, where is he?"

"Daisy you are safe. You are in a hospital," someone answers.

She opens her eyes and can see nurses in white clothes moving around her. She remembers. She was pregnant. She was carrying Lotus. Where is her huge belly? It is flat and feels light. Where is the baby?

Seeing her open her eyes, the nurse sitting by her side takes hold of her hands. "Daisy, how are you feeling?"

Daisy stares at her blankly and then mumbles, "Okay, I suppose, but where is my baby? Where is Tareq?"

"Your baby is fine," says the nurse, and then she softly asks, "Can you recall going somewhere in a car?"

Daisy's mind flips back to a vague picture of her and Tareq driving their car, of long winding highways, and then she distinctly hears Tareq's scream.

Tareq's screaming is hammering away in her head, louder and louder. She takes hold of her head with both hands, closes her ears to shut out the painful cries. And yet the screams echo back to her mind and then seem to tear her soul into pieces. In a flash it all comes back. They were going to Wilmington Beach, and they were in a head-on collision with another car coming from the opposite direction.

Ah, yes, she had heard Tareq's scream, and then in the blur of the moment she had seen Tareq's blood gushing from his smashed face, fresh blood bursting out in streams. Just before she herself had collapsed into a blank world, she had seen the bulging eyes, the vacant eyes, of Tareq, as if he were taking a last look at her.

Daisy stares at the blue eyes of the nurse, who is intently looking at her face, and she manages to whisper, "My husband, where is he?"

The nurse takes both of her hands in her own and every so softly says, "I know you will not rest until you know where he is, but the news is not good."

Daisy's heart turns as if she already knows what is coming, but she still whispers, dragging out the words, "Oh, how can he be gone?" Even though she does not want to hear the words, she is compelled to say them.

She hardly listens as the nurse says, "I am sorry, dear, but he went to Heaven at the moment of the collision. But don't you remember, you were pregnant? You have your baby, a beautiful girl. You are lucky to have the baby healthy and alive!"

Daisy stares at the nurse, a long disbelieving stare, and then begins to shake, whispering over and over again, "Tareq, dead? Tareq, dead? Tareq, dead?"

Her whispers continue, and then she is suddenly looking upward, as if she might see him somewhere on the ceiling, perhaps spot his spirit. Her eyes roll helplessly. She gives a long and loud scream and then faints.

Daisy's soul inside her goes berserk. She tries to put proper sense into Daisy, to make her able to accept the cruel truth. But when she comes to her senses, Daisy's mind is not in its proper functioning state. Her thoughts are crazy, no longer rational or calm. Daisy's soul tries to put peace into her, to help her accept Tareq's death. It urges her to be brave and tries to tell her that she needs to keep her sanity to look after Lotus. But the shock is winning over the soul, and Daisy is soon being transferred into a mental institution. She has to be treated for severe post-traumatic stress disorder. Consequently, there is a total resignation from Daisy's normal life: she is not speaking or talking to anyone.

Dancing Light keeps in constant touch with Daisy's soul. Under the critical circumstances, Dancing Light needs continuous advice. Lotus sleeps peacefully bundled in her baby cot at the hospital where she was born. Lotus is a beautiful child. She has inherited the fairness of Daisy's skin. Tareq's black hair and Daisy's blond is blended into a rich chestnut mass of hair she was born with. The wide red mouth, sharp nose, and brown eyes are placed on her face in a symmetry of all that is sweet. The doctors and nurses are all in love with the baby.

Lotus's heart is seeking the love of her mother and father. Every once in a while she starts crying. The nurse comes in and picks her up. The nurses are very kind, and they hold the fretful baby and comfort her.

"Shh...shh...," they croon in the baby's ears. "We are here to love you and hold you." They press Lotus against their bosoms until the warmth of the human touch calms her.

The nurses are doing their best, but Dancing Light is having a hard time consoling Lotus as she cries for her mother. Dancing Light allows a crooning voice to flow into the tender memory of Lotus. It is the voice Daisy used to sing to the unborn child. She rewinds her memory and replays more voices, so that Lotus can hear her mother talking to her from the heart.

"Hey, baby girl! You know that Mommy loves you?"

Lotus hears her mother's voice and is instantly comforted. Lotus whimpers and gurgles as if feeling happy and goes off to sleep. The nurses wonder if the angels are making her smile.

Dancing Light, still new in the world of human beings, cannot find an explanation for the Creator's decision to take away Tareq and make life so tragic.

"Why are these human beings being punished so by fate? Fate is controlled by the Creator," she asks Daisy's soul when it comes to hover near Lotus. Daisy's soul is trying to send messages to Daisy's brain, trying to filter through an image of the little girl, Lotus.

Daisy's soul sighs as if baffled and replies, "The Creator has strange ways of showing life to humans. Tareq's mother chose to have an abortion in her early life. Perhaps taking the son away from the mother was life's way of giving her a lesson. She had a baby blessed to her, but she chose to end its life. The Creator was not happy with that. Daisy's sufferings seem so unfair, but then life is often unfair. We cannot control fate."

Just then they can clearly see a spirit standing quietly near them, and with strong intuition they know that it is Tareq. His physical self is not clear, but an invisible yet strong powerful presence is there. Dancing Light knows that it is Lotus's father. He has come to see his baby daughter after his departed soul begged the Creator to allow him a look at his child.

The spirit talks to Dancing Light, saying, "My mother, Momota, is here. She came on the morning flight. She is there sitting by my grave and crying. But I will always be somewhere near Lotus. You can direct her thoughts toward me, and she will find peace in her heart. She can see me at times but will imagine that she is dreaming. You see people often have visions of us, but they do not realize we are spirits. Now I have to go, Ma will come here soon."

The voice of the father seems to touch the baby's heart, and she looks peaceful. Tareq's spirit kisses Lotus gently on the forehead before becoming a white form and stepping backward slowly, as if not wanting to go. And then the spirit quietly fades into nothing.

Dancing Light stares long at the vanishing spirit of Tareq. She promises that once Lotus is grown, gets married, and if some day she conceives, Dancing Light will ensure that she does not go for abortions. She is fearful of fate, which deals cruel blows in unexpected ways. She wonders what will happen to the baby with the father gone and the mother in a mental hospital.

fifteen

Daisy is still in the mental hospital where the doctors sent her after she withdrew from the life around her. She does not even ask about her baby. She sits quietly, at times holding a storybook and pretending to read. The nurses have tried to communicate by bringing her a laptop and getting her connected to social websites. Daisy's friends have informed the doctors of how she used Facebook all the time during the days of her pregnancy.

It is early morning. The weather is holding just the first hints of fall, and there is a cool crispness in the air. A month has passed since the accident, and Lotus is in the care of Daisy's friends and Momota, her grandmother, though she is still in hospital for the care she needs for being born prematurely. Momota is trying to gain custody of Lotus. Daisy's mother was at the funeral for Tareq and wanted to take Daisy and Lotus, but Momota convinced them she wanted to raise her granddaughter. However, Daisy has to stay in America for the time being for the doctors advise her not to travel just yet. Momota offers to help with the hospital bills. Daisy's mother and father refuse, saying that they will take care of Daisy and hope that Lotus will come to see her mother when she grows up. Tareq's death has opened their eyes to the reality that their daughter has lost the man she loved. Standing beside Lotus's baby cot Daisy's father murmurs softly, "I wish I could go back on time to be with Tareq and Daisy and be happy with them. Our arrogance was a mistake we cannot undo."

To take care of Lotus, Daisy's breast milk is being collected with a breast pump and brought for the baby everyday by Momota, as she juggles between hospitals and federal offices.

"What are you doing to me?" Daisy asks the nurses who use the pumps to collect the milk. On the doctor's advice, they have not introduced infant formulas to Lotus. Considering the mother's absence and the baby's health, it is important for the baby to have her mother's milk as long as possible.

Momota is ready to fight all the legal battles to take her granddaughter and raise her in Bangladesh. It is a tough and lengthy procedure, for by birth Lotus is a United States citizen. It takes almost two months to complete the paperwork while Momota stays with her relatives. Other Bangladeshi immigrants are helpful and give her rides to the different offices before she can take custody of Lotus and gain permission to take her to Bangladesh.

Dancing Light watches over Momota and Lotus. She wonders what kind of life she will have in Bangladesh.

Gradually Lotus is released from the hospital, and then Momota tries to reunite the child with her mother. But every time she takes Lotus to Daisy, the mother stares blankly at the little bundle and moves away, as if afraid of her own child.

"What is that, and who are you?" Daisy asks Momota.

Daisy does not allow her mother-in-law to come near her, and so from the door of her hospital room, Momota tries to connect to her.

"This is your baby, dear. Take her in your arms."

But Daisy turns around as if to avoid the sight of the little baby that whimpers softly when near the mother.

Dancing Light listens to Lotus. From time to time, Lotus seeks her mother, and Dancing Light has to ask the Creator to put peace into the baby's heart. She finds it difficult to do it all by herself. She seeks Tareq's spirit, hoping it will be nearby. And although she cannot see the spirit, Lotus often smiles suddenly and goes to sleep as if in her mother's arms. Dancing Light knows by instinct that it is the spirit's advocacy for the innocent baby.

As Dancing Light lies sleepless, she hears the Creator say, "You only have to ask for my help, and I will send it. Don't worry. I have angels guarding little Lotus, for orphans have a special place with me. While I have given them pain in life, I also guide them with a stronger heart."

Dancing Light is much relieved when Tareq's mother, finally obtaining custody of the baby, cuddles Lotus to her bosom and they snuggle happily.

"Strange," says Daisy's soul, who is near Dancing Light. "See the magic of the blood connection? Lotus seems to know that she is in the hands of her father's mother and feels an affinity for her."

Daisy's soul is talking to Dancing Light while Momota packs the little one's belongings. "Well, Lotus is flying to Bangladesh with her Grandma. But my time travel tells me that when Lotus gets her first job, she will try to take her mother back to Bangladesh."

Daisy's soul says to Dancing Light, "Well, you will be flying to Bangladesh tomorrow. When you are flying in those planes, you will feel nostalgic, for you will be in space, that layer of infinity close to the Land of Illumination. Maybe you will feel what humans call 'homesick.'"

Dancing Light watches Daisy's soul move away, and she feels a bit alone. But she knows that Daisy's soul will go to Lotus, even in Bangladesh, for a mother cannot fail her child, whether sane or not. In her soul, in her heart, and in her mind, the love is there.

"Love is the magic in human lives," concludes Dancing Light. She wonders how love will be working in Lotus's life. Will it bring her happy or sad chapters? Will smiles fill the pages, or will they be smeared tears?

Part Six

Horizon Day and Dancing Light's Story for Tareq's Spirit: Lotus in Bangladesh – Two- and- half- month Old and Onwards

sixteen

In the human world, it is a special night for the invisible beings. Spirits, souls, angels, and genies are gathered for a special meeting. This day is called Horizon Day. Though it is invisible beings that gather on this day, the meeting takes place in the human world. The name comes from the illusion of earth and sky meeting on the horizon. The invisible beings that are so much a part of the visible world are together, and yet human eyes cannot see them.

On this day they mingle and talk of the human world. Some give great stories of personal experiences. There are happy accounts and sad, and there are tales that confuse them. And yet all bow down to the Creator, knowing that they cannot control fate's strings tethering the humans.

Dancing Light has joined the meeting. She left Lotus sleeping peacefully in her cozy bedroom. In the warm summer night, the scents of flowers mingle on the gentle breeze. Up in the sky, a pale moon hangs as if smiling at the gathering of invisible beings. She finds a spirit representing Tareq waiting for her.

"Dancing Light, I have a request to make," the spirit says in the same gentle tone with which Tareq used to speak in life.

Dancing Light smiles at the spirit of her host's father and says, "You know I will do anything in my power to do as you say. Now tell me, how can I help you?"

"I want to have a complete picture of Lotus's life in Bangladesh. She was my only child, and her growing up in my motherland holds a profound part of me. I have been with her at times but I cannot be in peace without knowing all that has happened to her while she struggled to survive."

Dancing Light looks thoughtful for a moment and then says, "I can bring the story to you. You have to close your eyes, and I'll project the story of Lotus's life in Bangladesh like a motion picture to you. Although you will be seeing all the years she spent in your country, you will see it within a flash. Let's hope I can show you all. At times the Creator does not allow us to enter into time zones when he thinks it's for the best." Dancing Light takes hold of Tareq's spirit hands, as if to reach into its inner being, and says, "Close your eyes, and forget that I am here. Just focus on the images that come to your mind."

Tareq begins to see spirals of light at first, different colors blending into the stream of light. And then he sees his little girl. She has chestnut hair, just as he and Daisy had imagined she would. She has delicate fair skin, brown eyes, and a sharp nose set above perfectly shaped lips. There is such a strange resemblance to her mother! He wishes he could hold her in his arms. Tears well and spill over his cheeks as he stretches his eyes to find her, and there like a rising sun, his little daughter appears. She is a baby, then a little girl, then a teenager, and then a young woman. Stage by stage she is growing in her life in Bangladesh….

⊷✵⊶

Lotus, the two-and-half-month old baby Dida brought home needs motherly care. Dida feeds the baby goat's milk, for she knows it is good for digestion. She does not like the available baby milk products in the shops, as they are often adulterated. Dida has given up looking after the little farm she used to run so that she can be with the baby full time. Instead she leases the lands for growing crops. It is not till Lotus is almost two years old that the woman starts looking after her farm again.

Lotus as a little girl learned to speak Bangla from her grandmother as her first language. She calls her grandmother "Dida," coming from "Dadi" which is what Bangladeshis call their paternal grandmothers. Dida leaves no stone unturned in order to have her granddaughter educated. Living in Moinatori, the village in Manikganj, makes it a difficult task. She has limited access to the educational facilities of Dhaka, the capital city. Dida was widowed fifteen years back, and so she has to bring up Lotus all on her own. Her income from the farmland and the annual crops help her to run her village home. The rent from a house that Tareq had built in Dhaka helps her to provide the best education for her granddaughter that she can while remaining in the village.

Dida, now in her late fifties, has salt-and-pepper curly hair that frames her sweet face. As far back as Lotus can remember, Dida's lips have been stained red from the chewing of beetle nuts and the leaves that she calls "paan." Lotus never feels any dearth of love and affection growing up with her grandmother. The lady allows freedom for the teenager, freedom to grow into the best of her being. There are times when the villagers say, "Why do you pamper Lotus so much? Give her away in marriage as soon as you can. You will be relieved when Lotus has her own family."

But Dida is very firm about educating Lotus and always replies, "Why, my granddaughter has to earn her master's degree before she gets married. I will not have her depending on her husband. She is intelligent and can go far in life. I'm sure my son would have spared no effort to educate his daughter."

She keeps to her word, and as soon as Lotus completes her schooling up to tenth grade in the village, she is sent off to the capital city, Dhaka, to continue her education.

◦◊◦

Here Dancing Light pauses in the story and says, "I will not go through her education in Dhaka, but from here on you will see the story without pause."

"But isn't her student life important?" asks Tareq's spirit.

"Of course the whole life story of each is an epic of its own. But in my time travel, I have to choose which chapters to show, for I may not be able to see her story if the Creator suddenly decides to stop my time travel. And so I think its best you watch the story as I present it to you." Dancing Light goes on, and Tareq once again closes his eyes and continues to see Lotus's life in Bangladesh.

In her numerous letters to Lotus living in boarding schools, Dida always ends with, "Do not worry about money. Take the classes you want, and if you need tutors, go to them. Remember you are investing in your whole life."

Lotus knows very well that while her grandmother is sending her money for her education, she herself is spending as little as she can on herself. At the end of each day, Lotus promises to herself that she will make it up to her once she completes her education and has a job. Lotus never fails to thank the stars for having Dida in her life. The gentle, kind lady has been her guiding light, her source of love and strength forever. Often she hugs Dida and plants kisses on the soft cheeks, saying over and over, "You are my world, you are my life. Don't ever go far away from me, for then I'll not live anymore."

Dida tussles Lotus's hair playfully and says, "You are my life too, and so how could I go far away from you?" But in her heart she feels a little worried that Lotus seems to feel insecure after losing her father and not having her mother with her. Both Dida and Lotus want to bring Daisy to Bangladesh as soon as possible.

Thankfully, days are easier now and when vacations come, Lotus takes the first bus to come back to Dida. She saves each and every penny she can for the bus fare on the weekends. And the hard days are more or less over, and with her bachelor's degree in accounting, Lotus is already working in a well-established bank in the heart of Dhaka. She is twenty-five years old and has grown into a glamorous young lady. With her good looks, she makes heads turn wherever she goes.

seventeen

On one such weekend trip, Lotus sits upon the riverbank. The river is called Jamuna, and it runs very close by her home. It is her favorite place to relax in her village of Moinatori. It is in Mankganj, near Dhaka, the capital of Bangladesh. Though she has never seen her father, the village where he lived seems to bring him nearer to her. The serenity of village life sprawling before her brings peace to her heart. She often imagines her father sitting near the river in his time. Dida has told her that before he left for the United States to get his master's degree, he used to come here often and watch the river.

Under the sunlight the river glistens as it winds around the villages. The villages are surrounded by trees along the bank. Lotus can hear contentment in the murmuring of the water as the current rushes along with the river's long, long journey to the sea. Lotus can almost hear a voice in the murmur of the water, laughing away as the force of the water causes landslides along the bank.

"The beauty of the river is like a mirage," murmurs Lotus.

Though the river looks beautiful, there is danger in its overflowing the bank. Lotus is reminded of a folk song she had heard her grandmother often hum:

> *Rivers flow in glee.*
> *Listen, humans cry.*
> *No, no it will not stop,*

But go on and on,
Till it meets its love,
And falls into arms of the sea.

It is a popular song of the villagers, who are helpless against the disasters nature can bring. At the whim of the weather, thousands of people may have their lands flooded, their crops and houses destroyed, and lose their animals. A flood can make their struggle for survival the worst of its kind. They never have enough cash to buy food.

Thinking about money, Lotus's mind veers to the pending bills from the mental hospital where Daisy is hospitalized. Immediately after getting her job, Lotus went to the United States and brought her mother to Bangladesh. Momota was very generous and helped with all the expenses to bring Daisy over. Lotus knows that it was done out of the small savings from Dida's farm. She can never thank Dida enough for all she does.

After arriving in Dhaka with her mother, Lotus tried to keep her mother in her apartment. But Daisy is so ill that twice Lotus is just in time to take away the kitchen knives with which her mother tries to slit her wrists. The psychiatrist in the United States had said that going to Bangladesh, her dead husband's home, might worsen her depression. And it seems that the doctor was right, for Daisy became more depressed right after coming to Bangladesh.

At times she mumbles under her breath, "Dhaka, Tareq, baby…Tareq…."

It is impossible to be at home with her mother, since Lotus has to go to work every day. She tries keeping a nurse, but Daisy will not communicate with the lady. So the hospital is the only choice left to her.

Dancing Light is always trying to tune Lotus's heart to harmony and urging her to go and do things she likes. While Lotus watches the boats sail slowly on the river, a sudden drizzle passes over, leaving the grasses wet and soggy around her.

It seems as though the rain has come by mistake. It stops within minutes, and the sun is quick to show its face, bright and sparkling as if victorious over the clouds. Lotus is sitting upon a small boulder under the afternoon sun. She notices the tiny flowers around her. They are only shrubs, but they have beautiful purple and yellow flowers. Even the blades of grass hold delicate white flowers. Each and every life of the Creator seems to be eager to expose itself. She is thinking of how she too is trying to make life meaningful in her own way.

"Nature blends into a life" is Dida's favorite saying when she talks of nature. Living in the village, she is fond of nature, and Lotus often sees her talking to trees as if they understand her.

Lotus sometimes says, "Dida, the trees understand your Bangla, but will they understand me if I talk to them in English?"

Dida, being a witty lady, answers, "Well, they understand whatever language you use. It's the language of the heart that nature understands. Be silent and touch them, and you will feel connected."

Sitting beside the river, Lotus finds a similarity between her life and the tiny flowers around her. Like them, she too is trying to shine through the hectic life she leads. Hearing a voice calling her, she turns around. It is her childhood friend, Husna. Now a mother of four, Husna looks older than her age. Lotus motions her to come and sit by her, saying, "Husna, how are you? Why don't you take care of yourself? Look at you, so thin and unkempt!"

"When did you come?" asks Husna, coming closer but refusing to sit. "Lotus, won't you get married? Look at you getting to be an old maid," Husna teases playfully.

Lotus gets up and takes her friend's hands into her own, saying, "That is life, you know? Look at you, the mother goose, married at the age of fifteen and having four kids. And I'm still waiting for a prince charming."

"You're lucky that your grandmother educated you. We had no choice. Our parents thought of us as burdens until we got married," Husna remarks a little sadly.

After a bit of gossiping about their other friends, Husna is on her way, saying she has to prepare dinner or else her little one will fall asleep. Lotus settles down once again in her place and falls back to her reverie.

Meeting Husna reminds her that remaining a virgin at twenty-five years of age is like living out of modern society. Her other friends are already married or at least have fiancés. These days young girls in Bangladesh often lost their virginity as teenagers. And drugs, alcohol, smoking, premarital sex, every temptation is there. And yet the truth remains buried for fear of social repercussions. Scandals are common among the elites, but the media is often silenced from reporting on the corruption of the common by strong hands behind the scenes.

As memories sweep over Lotus, Dancing Light keeps Lotus peaceful and at times whispers to her heart, "Lotus, there is one person I don't want you to remember. That would ruin the whole weekend."

But in the back of her mind, Lotus is already thinking of that person and trying not to let him break her peace. Sitting in this place, there are times when she recalls the most wonderful moments of life and sometimes the worst, but all are recorded on the riverbank. The memories seem to swing back and forth, one trying to gain purchase over the other.

"I am important," says a string of memories, speaking of the day she found the first red rose blooming in her garden. Just then another string of memories steps in to say, "Ah no, I'm the more important one. I am the star of her world of memories, because within me lives her first kiss of life."

First kiss.... The very thought of the incident has her blushing, and the very person Dancing Light has been trying to put off springs from her memories, like a streak of unwanted light from a passing car when you are trying to sleep. It is the memory of something that happened some time ago, something she desperately wishes to forget. An image of a young man, rugged and handsome, emerges in her heart. It is Bijoy. Who could forget the name of their first love, the one who gave the first kiss on the very first date? Lotus had fallen in love with Bijoy for his spontaneous nature. He was like the spring breeze, playing around the trees, and with each touch he was bringing a new flower. Lotus was used to long planning in her life and so Bijoy with his impulsiveness was a refreshing change. He took her to places, bought her gifts, kissed and cuddled her as if those were the most natural things of his life.

Ghostlike voices start ringing in her ears. They come from the first day she met Bijoy through a friend. Lotus was then in the university, working hard for her bachelor's degree. Memory of the first happy encounter soon gets clouded with dark veils and Lotus slips into a bleak mood. Her heart and mind are at war, the heart bathing in sorrow and the mind trying to make her accept the betrayal without further struggle, telling her, "There is no use holding on to the past. Just let it go."

Dancing Light tries to keep the unpleasant memories at bay. But the wounded heart hears a male voice going on and on. "Lotus, I love you. Lotus, you mean everything to me!" And then again the same voice comes but with words of poison. They make Lotus cringe even after so many years. Lotus puts both of her palms against her ears, as if to stop the voice. And yet mercilessly, the words penetrate her psyche, for words of love and betrayal may pass through the ears, but they find their ground in the heart and the soul.

"I don't believe you love me. Your career means more to you than me. Well, I cannot wait forever! This is the last day I will see or talk to you," the male voice shouts when Lotus refuses get married just when he wants to.

Is this angry, obstinate voice emanating from the same man who sung of love all those days? Lotus had been too stunned to say anything when the love of her life banged the door shut after spreading the venom of love gone sour. He had broken her heart, made her world a nasty place, just when she was putting up her head, fighting all odds in a tough, male-dominated society.

Dancing Light calls out to Daisy's soul as Lotus begins to cry silently. "What can I do to make her forget that rascal who betrayed her love and trust?"

Daisy's soul thinks for a while and says, "Sometimes it is good to have a cry. Let her cry, and she will feel her heart lighten. The Creator will help her get through. He helps people who are wronged, but love is something different. One cannot coerce it, nor is it something one can forget just because a part of one wants to."

Lotus softly recites a stanza from her favorite poem, "For Love's Sake," by Susan Christensen.

I'm so tired of this empty feeling
I'm so tired of being alone
I lay here staring at the ceiling
Waiting by the phone

I jump when the phone rings…
It brings a smile to my face
When he hangs up my heart strings
And I sink back into my lonely place

I wish and I dream
That we'll be together soon
I can't wait until we can look up hand in hand
At the stars and at the moon

I yearn for his kisses
His touch - His embrace
I can't wait for Thursdays
When I get to see his face

I'm flooded with thoughts of him
In my heart, soul, and mind
I imagine his touch
So gentle and kind

I try not to weep
I hope he doesn't hear my cries
But I can't stop the tears
Falling from my eyes

I cry a thousand tears
And think - how much more can I take?
But in my heart I know I'd wait a thousand years
All for love's sake.

Sad memories delve into the dark corners of the past and link themselves to the present. And there are memories, which at times stand as one. Images of Bijoy and her holding hands and walking, sharing ice cream from the same cup, pass through her mind and cloud her peace of mind.

Lotus shakes her head, dispelling briefly the darkness that had taken hold. Thinking that Dida must be missing her, Lotus stands up to stretch her hands and feet. Sighing deeply she sort of adds up the last unhappy thoughts, saying to herself, "Bijoy, you hurt me so badly! Yet why can't I erase you from my heart?"

In those difficult days she had said to Bijoy, "Look I need to get things together. I've just got my sick mother in a hospital, and there is a huge amount of loan to be paid very soon. Dida needs a lot of medications and constant doctor's checkups at this age. I just need to catch my breath."

Bijoy scoffed and said, "Oh sure, everything is more important than what I want. I can't wait for you forever!"

How love makes or breaks a heart, Lotus ponders. Her grandmother is insisting that she get married and settle down. But she has put the idea of marriage out of her mind. She is not for relationships yet. Bijoy has an ego problem typical of the village men in Bangladesh. It is Dancing Light who has shown Lotus that she has her own choices in life and helps her stick to her decision to get married later on.

When Bijoy urged her to give up her job and marry him, to settle down like a village woman, Dancing Light showed Lotus that what he wanted was selfish, that he was not at all caring about the things Lotus values in life. Daisy's soul was in constant touch, helping Dancing Light keep Lotus on the right track.

Daisy's soul often advises Dancing Light. "Remind Lotus again and again that she is a US citizen by birth, and she can go back to the great land if she is not happy here. I am sure she will want to go and see her father's grave very soon. Just keep the dream alive in her."

The sun is low in the sky and spreading its last hues with a splendor of colors over the river. The water is bathed with brilliant scarlet and purple. It glistens as the evening breeze teases the waves into chasing one another. "Well, bye, Jamuna. I have to go now." Lotus speaks to the river as if it is a human being.

She wants to sit near Dida and talk to her awhile before starting on her way to Dhaka. She is feeling guilty about leaving her grandmother alone. The old lady is always waiting for Lotus to come to the village home. Both of them share news about Dhaka and the village when Lotus returns, talking late into the night while Dida gently runs her fingers through Lotus's hair. Her loving touch always puts Lotus fast to sleep, and then Dida too eventually drifts off.

As Lotus meanders through the green fields, making her way slowly back to Dida, Lotus begins thinking of all the wonderful people in her life. "Your life is an unfortunate love story, and you are the desperate heroine," her friend and roommate in Dhaka, Chaiti, often tries to console her. At times Chaiti will say, "Come on, Didi, speak your heart, you can call him. Cry, shout, and call him all the names you want over the phone. If you go over and tell him how cruel he is you will feel so good."

Though Lotus never did call Bijoy, thinking of Chaiti and the way she calls her Didi, (sister), makes Lotus smile. She is lucky to have Chaiti with her, so loyal and loving. Thinking of her roommate, Lotus remembers she has to be back to Dhaka by the evening bus, meaning she must hurry home to pack. She hastens her steps. Many passengers would be returning to work in the busy metropolitan city after the weekend. Among them would be Chaiti, who lives in the next village, and the engineer Rajiv, who is courting Chaiti. The couple has been seeing each other for some time. Though they live in the nearby villages of Moinatori, they met in Dhaka. She hopes Chaiti will be happy with her love.

Lotus greets the villagers she passes on the way home. Here almost everybody knows everybody. Her slender figure looks attractive in a T-shirt and jeans. But she always has a neck scarf when she comes to the village. Her mother's fairness and her father's Bangladeshi sweetness have blessed her with a mystic beauty. Her large eyes are lined with kohl and her wide generous mouth outlined with lipstick.

"Do you know what a stunning beauty you are?" says a passing youth she knows has feelings for her.

This is a compliment she heard often while she was in North Carolina, bringing her mother to Bangladesh. It is her complexion that is so captivating as a result of the mixed parentage. When she reaches home, Dida remarks, "Lotus, is your river dearer than me? Could you not have sat near me for longer before you leave?"

As Lotus kisses her grandmother good-bye, she is thinking that when it comes to being with the loved ones, you can never be close enough for long. She is already planning her next visit to Dida.

eighteen

Back in Dhaka, life begins in full earnest for Lotus. Juggling between home and office seems to fill the days. Working in a multinational bank is no easy job. Most days it is late in the evening when she returns home. Lotus shares a small apartment with Chaiti. It is one of those small apartments that have recently sprung up like mushrooms in the growing city. Each of the two rooms has only enough space to set a bed and a small table. But the rooms have built-in closets, and the kitchens are well equipped with cupboards. The rent is too much for Lotus to pay by herself, but with Chaiti sharing the utility bills and rent, things are much easier.

Chaiti and Lotus both like the location of their house, in the heart of the city, and there is greater privacy living in the apartment. The women have their individual bedrooms, and the landlady, Lily, living on another floor of the same building, seldom bothers them. At a cheaper rate they could have gone to the working-women's hostel, but both are privacy lovers, and a great deal would have to be sacrificed to live in a boarding house. So they pay a little extra for what they love.

In addition, these apartments have security guards. They have to pay for that too, but not much when compared to the ease and comfort of the system. The landlady was reluctant at first to allow unmarried young ladies into her apartment building. But Chaiti, master at the art of flattery, repeated "Auntie dear" at least a hundred times while smiling sweetly, trying to convince the lady.

"Look, Auntie dear, we're the new generation of working women, and we face so many challenges already. We can't find good matches for husbands, so where can we live? If you, so motherly and kind, do not help out, how will we work to support ourselves?"

They visited Lily at least three or four times, and gradually the landlady agreed, saying , "Look, usually I do not lease to single men or women, but you two seem to be sweet and honest. I will have the contract signed just for one year, and if things work out, I will renew it."

Chaiti and Lotus both hugged her in turn, and the landlady has signed the lease contract every year for four years now. In fact, whenever they run into each other, she says, "Why don't you two get yourselves husbands? Soon you will be joining those old maids' groups."

"Auntie, we are waiting for our Prince Charmings. It seems our heroes are late," Chaiti replies to the landlady, knowing that she means well.

Lotus and Chaiti love to have dinner together. The one to come home earliest waits for the other, and they share the day's news over their meal. Lunch is always taken at the office, and they share the cooking of the other meals and snacks by alternating weeks. Grocery shopping follows the same routine. Sharing makes life rather fun, in spite of the hectic weeks they run.

Chaiti often sings self-composed offbeat songs about the weekends in Bangladesh. They always begin on Fridays. At times she takes the fry pan and beats it like a drum as she sings:

> *Friday, Friday,*
> *Saturday, Saturday,*
> *We're happy, we're gay*
> *Bussing to our villages*
> *Up and away, up and away.*

"Where did you get this new word, *bussing*?" Lotus asks one day.

Chaiti gives a chuckle and quick smile before replying, "It's new, self-made English, Didi. We ride busses, and so it's *bussing*."

Most of the busy weeks culminate in happy weekend trips to Moinatori. They usually board the bus toward home with singing hearts and return with them heavy. Leaving home is never easy. Sometimes Chaiti stays back when Rajiv and she have plans of their own. They have recently been giving thoughts to marriage. When they are together, Lotus always calls them "lovebirds."

In the evenings, Lotus is usually the first one to come home. She has some time to herself before Chaiti comes in with the latest news of her boyfriend and all that is hot in the city. Chaiti, who works at a newspaper, is usually able to spend some time with Rajiv even after meeting all her deadlines.

Lotus often says, "Chaiti, I don't need to watch any news on TV or read a newspaper. I just wait for you to come home, the chattering bulletin of the town."

Chaiti gives her big hugs and exclaims, "You cannot bar me from chattering away to my heart's content and meeting my fiancé. Aw, that is like suffocating me."

To Chaiti, first comes her Rajiv and then comes everything else. But to Lotus, her own beliefs and values come with equal strides, and this was reason enough not to get married just because Bijoy wanted it. She had been shocked at how egotistical the man could be.

Dida tried to insist that she get married as Bijoy wished. But Lotus had seen how her grandmother had toiled away at home, saving each penny. Since her grandfather died a long while back, money had become a constant hardship for the old lady.

"Money! I will earn a lot and let my grandmother spend it lavishly. How she has sacrificed for me," Lotus vowed to herself after she joined the bank.

An American sense of freedom is ingrained in her personality, and she is firm in working herself up the ladders of life. She seems to sense her father's spirit guarding her as she moves around Dhaka, a place that is full of unexpected troubles like accidents, scams, and muggings.

As Lotus tries to balance her office, home, and taking care of Dida and Daisy, she often stares up at the sky and wonders if even its vastness can hold all her troubles. She mutters, "Even if life holds the troubles like Pandora's box, I will hold on to hope and keep going."

nineteen

Lotus hails a rickshaw, the three wheelers that rove in thousands on the streets of Dhaka. It is a weekday, and she is on her way home after a stressful day at the office. She consoles herself, saying, "Two more days to go and then comes the weekend."

She wonders if Chaiti is interested in watching a movie at the cinema complex in Bashundhara. That is the only decent place where two young women can go alone without risking hecklers lurking all around. She feels insecure, knowing that the abuse of women is on the rise, even though more and more women are joining the working force. Males seem to be taking the added advantage of having more working women in the city by harassing them. Policemen often stand by while uncouth young men tease groups of female garment workers. The women know safety comes in numbers.

Back at home Lotus sits sipping a cup of hot coffee and turning her thoughts over to the past few days. Chaiti's loud and boisterous laughter sails in through the front door. Lotus hears her roommate opening the front door. Hearing her chattering away, Lotus assumes that Rajiv is with her. Lotus does not like the idea of having boyfriends over to the apartment. After all, their society is still a very conservative one, and it is better to save one's skin by being cautious. However, she gives into Rajiv coming because the young man, like Chaiti, calls her "Didi" and treats her like an elder sister.

Just then Chaiti enters the room with Rajiv, who follows her with hesitant steps. He gives Lotus a disarming smile when their eyes meet. "Sorry to come in unannounced. But you see, I am taking Chaiti out for her birthday treat, and since it's already dark outside, Chaiti thought you would want her escorted at all times."

Lotus gives him a quick smile and says, "Rajiv, have you ever come in without an excuse to be with Chaiti? Your excuses are always ready."

As she is talking to Rajiv, she gets up and goes to her room to get the birthday gift she has ready for Chaiti. Chaiti had treated her to lunch earlier in the month on her birthday. Rajiv gives a short laugh and says, "I know you are kind, Didi, and will not keep me standing outside the door."

Before Chaiti moved in, Lotus laid down the ground rules for their apartment. Rule number one is *no boyfriends*. The rest include keeping the restroom clean, cooking only on weekends, and not playing loud music after eight in the evening. Lotus had written these rules down and placed them on the refrigerator with a magnet that said, "Life is great to share."

Rule number one was broken, but Chaiti follows the others. Lotus thinks it is nice of Chaiti to look upon her as an elder sister and abide by the "dos and don'ts." Lotus's often smiles to herself when she realizes that Chaiti uses the rules to suit her own needs. She and Rajiv always find loopholes allowing them to share time in the apartment.

Dancing Light watches as Lotus goes about her life as a working woman. This evening she is in tune with the humorous mood of Lotus, but she is puzzled over something strange about Rajiv. She calls out to Rajiv's soul and asks, "Hey, friend, why do I get a different vibe from your host? It's as if he does not really belong here. I mean in this country."

Rajiv's soul is always happy to be in touch with someone from the Land of Illumination. Usually Dancing Light and Rajiv's soul cannot talk much, for Chaiti is continually chattering and Rajiv's soul has to be attentive to the love of his host. But the soul explains to Dancing Light, saying, "You see, you don't feel so comfortable around me because Rajiv happens to be a test-tube baby. In fact, his mother received another man's sperm to make her pregnant. His father's sperm just was not doing its job, and so they went to Singapore to have science help them conceive. That is why he has a foreign touch about him. Maybe, because you yourself are from the United States, you feel the difference all the more. At times I have difficulty in getting Rajiv and Chaiti connected, because the girl is 101 percent Bengali. I just don't know how to connect, as the Creator did not disclose the genes of his unknown father to me."

"But the man who gave the sperm, surely his soul is somewhere out there. Doesn't he want to keep track of a son he has fathered?"

"These human beings are strange creatures. The biological father is totally out of the scene, happy just to have gotten some money for his sperm. And look at other divorced parents, fighting over their children's custody, even killing each other. And yet this man is indifferent to a child he has fathered."

"Didn't you have problems in the emotional transfer from his original father? I mean doesn't the lovemaking and the intense feelings between husbands and wives have anything to do with having a healthy baby? Rajiv's legal father did not give the sperm. Does that affect in any way how he loves the child?" Dancing Light asks.

Rajiv's soul gives a sharp laugh, saying, "Not at all, the father loves the child just as much as his own. You see, invisible history is made here. A Bangladeshi mother has Chinese ancestors' genes passed to the baby through the sperm donor. Who knows, maybe the force of Rajiv's genes will take him back to China."

Dancing Light chuckles loudly. "My, my, what a strange world the humans live in. I hope I return to the Land of Illumination with my sanity. Even my host with her American genes feels the impulse to live the American life. One day I found her day dreaming of a handsome man who will dance the waltz with her. And at times she even hums the "Star Spangled Banner," the American national anthem. You should see how she swoons over the American friends she has on Facebook."

"What happens when you feel tugs from your original family on her mother's side in America?" Rajiv's soul asks Dancing Light. "The blood connection is supposed to work wonders and build invisible love lines."

"Ah, at times I do have problems balancing Lotus with her Bengali moods and giving her a touch of her American ties. However, the Creator sends in angels, and at times genies, to help me out." Dancing Light replies.

While Dancing Light is having her chat, Lotus is busy pouring Rajiv a bowl of salted peanuts. She wants to be stricter with Chaiti about bringing Rajiv home, fearing the landlady. So she often says to the young man, "Rajiv, you know I would never keep you out, but try to keep your visits for special occasions. You know we have to earn our respect here. I am sure the landlady has objections to a young man dropping in at an apartment of single women too often."

"Oh, yes, I am aware and will be more careful, Didi. Don't worry."

"No offence meant, of course," Lotus says as she rises to offer him the coffee she has brewed in the coffee maker.

Rajiv smiles saying, "I'm glad we can work out things with you, Didi."

Just then Chaiti enters, twirling her fancy purse above her head. She is dressed in a lovely blue *sari*, and her thick shoulder-length hair beautifully frames her perfectly oval face. Her large eyes look lovely with eyeliner, and her full lips pout under mocha lipstick.

She takes sips from Rajiv's coffee and giving him a slap on his back, she says, "Rajiv, let's get going. All of us have work tomorrow. Didi, I am off." And with that she plants a kiss on Lotus's check.

Lotus gives her a pat on the back and says jokingly, "There goes your lipstick all over my cheeks."

Chaiti opens the front door, walking with short steps, tapping her high heels on the mosaic floor. With a last winning smile to Lotus, she steps through the door. Rajiv hurriedly takes a last sip of coffee and follows her.

As both of them stand together by the door for a moment, Lotus is thinking that they indeed make a lovely couple. It is as if they are made for each other. Rajiv is tall and handsome, with a slightly blunt nose and slanted eyes that seem to give hints of an unknown Chinese link. His eyes are dark but very sensible looking. Chaiti is tall too but is very fair and has lovely green eyes. Green eyes are not so common among Bangladeshis. Chaiti has a frailty about her, which seems to find calmness within Rajiv's firm masculine frame. Often Lotus notices how deeply and seriously Rajiv looks into Chaiti's flirting eyes. The girl gives one the impression that she is not serious about anything, yet within her is one of the strongest girls Lotus has ever met.

Bidding them both good-bye, Lotus settles down with the novel she has recently borrowed from the British Council Library. It's *The Horse Whisperer* by Nicolas Evans. Soon, however, her eyelids are drooping. Feeling drowsy after the stress of the long day, she puts down her book and heads toward her room. She keeps the light on in the hall so that Chaiti does not tumble in the darkness when she returns.

twenty

The weekdays seem to simply fly by, and soon it is the weekend again. Fridays and Saturdays are good days for going to the village or just lazing around. Chaiti has taken the weekend to go someplace with Rajiv, and Lotus is alone in the apartment. Lotus always finds the fact that Fridays and Saturdays constitute the weekend in Bangladesh strange, given that the greater world has Saturdays and Sundays off. It means the country remains cut off from the rest of the world for three days instead of the normal two.

Lotus curls up on the sofa beside the window, planning to spend this particular Friday finishing *The Horse Whisperer*. She is enjoying her story book and is looking forward to a few sublime hours of escapism. Reading novels is something she loves very much, but she is having second thoughts about acquiring a Kindle. Technology is certainly tempting, offering ease and comfort, and it would be much easier to carry the Kindle instead of heavy books in her handbag, but she loves the feel of the pages under her fingers.

"Once you read the book, get into the emotions, you no longer enjoy the movie," Lotus mumbles to herself, remembering the movie based on *The Horse Whisperer*. The story makes her heart hurt for the hero of the story, who dies at the end.

Here she begins to think of Bijoy yet again. He was her hero in the past for a time. She does not want to remember him, but it is like broken strings vibrating at odd frequencies. His spontaneity had won her heart but his withdrawal, similarly impulsive had filled her with bitterness. She cannot help it, for the man had once roused all her passions, only to sadly vanish from her life. The thought of their romance makes her glance up from her book and look at the sky through the open window. The infinity of the sky never fails to fill her heart with wonder. It always fills her heart with peace and hope, even when her heart is wallowing in the gutter.

Rising from her seat, Lotus opens the window of her room. Floating clouds in the sky always remind her of her own being. It is as if the clouds cannot find their way home and so are destined to continuously float along through life. She feels an empathy with these lost clouds. Her mind and heart also seem unable to find their home in the world.

At such times Dancing Light, to make her feel glad, gives her special life boosts, reminding her of the pleasure of being alive. Dancing Light makes Lotus focus more on the aesthetic senses and guides her to blend her life with nature. Imperfection is a way of life, and it has a beauty of its own. She gives Lotus the strength to bear the missing pieces in her life.

Though her father's physical presence in her life will always be vacant, her mother's is not. Lotus often wonders what life would have been if her mother had recognized her own daughter and demonstrated a little love and affection. At times, Daisy smiles a sad but very loving smile when Lotus visits her. Other times she looks at the beautiful young lady blankly, as if she has no idea why Lotus has come to see her at all.

Lotus feels like screaming out, "Mom, I love you! Can't you see through the haze to your own baby?" She wonders if that would shake her out of her stupor.

At such moments Dancing Light gets in touch with Daisy's soul and asks her, "How can you go on living when your host is so depressed all the time? Don't you feel like having some laughter and life?"

Daisy's soul always answers, "We are the Creator's servants, assigned to the body in which we are put. Daisy is crazy with grief, but that does not mean the Creator will take me away from her.

I'll have to be with her in her smiles and tears as long as she is in this world. Even in her insanity, I have to keep the flute of life playing for her."

Dancing Light listens and knows that Daisy's soul is passing on life lessons to her indirectly.

twenty-one

⚜

Alone on the weekend and feeling the need for some fresh air, Lotus takes out a chair and settles on the small balcony. Her thoughts flicker back and forth to Bijoy even after the nearly five years since their breakup. But Dancing Light is trying to divert Lotus to other thoughts, to bring peace to her heart. But alas Lotus's mind goes on flashing memories, and even her heart starts grumbling over the problems of life. A silent war rages between reason and passion in the seat of her soul. But these days Lotus gives momentary thoughts to other young men she meets occasionally, wonders if there can be a second man soon coming in to replace the old thoughts.

Dancing Light knows that Lotus still loves Bijoy somewhere deep inside. First love in a person's life holds a place as firm as a boulder in the sea, despite all the emotional turbulences it may bring. No matter how deeply you may be hurt by another person, first love somehow remains, like a sleeping shadow, waking every once in a while to soak the heart with renewed tenderness. She hums a song by Kazi Nazrul Islam, a giant Bangla literary figure, and taps the floor with her toes,

...*mor prothom moner mukul, jhore gelo hai...* (...the first bud of my heart has withered...)

Dancing Light feels frustrated at times like this, when human emotions become too strong and she cannot lead them as she wishes. So Lotus goes on reminiscing about her old love, until Dancing Light at last is able to move her thoughts to new possibilities. She urges Lotus to open Facebook and get lost in her friends and messages.

What a blessing this Internet is. Dancing Light is happy too, for strange as it may seem, at times she is able to get in touch with the others' souls as Lotus chats with them. For Dancing Light, it is fun to ask questions of Lotus's friends as their hosts chat. Through this she is able to know what is going on around other parts of the world.

The other day, Dennis, a Facebook friend of Lotus in America, was saying, "We are gypsies, you know. We move around as if the roads are our home. At times we may grow our own vegetables and fruits and tend cows for fresh milk for a while and then we move again."

"What does it mean? Does that mean you have no money?" Dancing Light prompted Lotus to ask Dennis.

"Ah, we are not poor but we choose to live a different life."

Dancing Light so far has not seen richness in her life and is surprised that people can have money and yet choose to move around instead of settling down with houses and cars.

During these chats, Dancing Light always holds the ulterior motive of trying to link someone to Lotus's heart over the Internet. Souls on the Internet tell her that people date and marry after connecting on the Internet.

A few days back, when Lotus was on the Internet, Dancing Light searched for a character called "Cupid," to ask him to shoot the arrows of love for Lotus.

But Dennis's soul laughed at her when she asked him about Cupid, and he said, "Cupid is a mythological character who matches young men and women together. But you cannot find his soul, for it lives in man's imagination only. True life with a soul comes only from the Creator."

However, Dennis's soul became serious as he added, "Love is a Heavenly gift, and only the Creator can stir up the feelings of a heart. Love can save lives, and love can destroy lives. This strong emotion is controlled by the Creator. Roam around and you will see people in love praying to him to unite them with their lost loves. But I have a problem."

Lotus is about to get up and close down Facebook, but Dancing Light urges her to stay on a little longer so that she and Dennis's soul can go on talking. She wants to know about this problem.

"You see, I have done the forbidden thing. I have fallen in love with an angel. She came down when Dennis's sister died, and she stayed with the mother until the funeral. She is so sweet and gentle. She comes when Dennis's mother cries for her daughter, and I get to see her," confesses Dennis's soul.

Dancing Light is awestruck and stammers, "I had no idea that souls can fall in love on their own with other invisible beings. I have heard of souls being in love with their hosts, but a soul in love with an angel? What will happen to you?" she asks quivering.

"No idea at all. I just hope we can make a request to the Creator to transfer me to the angel's world if I cannot love her as a soul."

Dennis's soul has Dancing Light even more confused about the human world. Dancing Light often wonders if a second man will come into Lotus's life. There were two or three men who tried to become close to her, tried to win her heart, but every time she tried beginning a relationship with them, Bijoy seemed to stand in between them. In the deepest planes of Lotus's heart, she fears they will all be like Bijoy—betrayers. Chaiti often reminds her that it was not fair to expect two persons to be alike.

"Trust me in this, Didi, two persons cannot be alike. And you know what? You loved that man, and he left you anyway. Why do you want another one like him? Personally, I don't think you need anyone the likes of Bijoy in your life again. Someone completely different is the man you want, to wipe out all bad memories.

With the weekend getting along, Lotus is in a pensive mood and enjoying the quietness of her home. Chaiti is off with Rajiv for the weekend, visiting some friends in another town. Sitting on the balcony and looking over the buildings sprawling in front of her, she is reminded of how densely populated Dhaka is becoming. She watches people moving about on the streets below. It seems as if they have to keep themselves ever-vigilant simply to avoid bumping into each other.

Saturday is spent quietly with books, giving her time to reminisce about her past and ponder the present. There comes with a call from Dida on the cell phone while she is still in bed. Lotus has her grandmother's picture on the display screen of her iPhone.

"Good morning, Lo," Dida says. "Are you coming next weekend?"

Lotus smiles over the phone as she listens to impatience in Dida's voice. She gently replies, "Dida, you know that I will come since I am not seeing you this weekend."

"Good," says Dida, adding, "I am getting some coconut cakes ready for you and just want to make sure that you will come."

Lotus smiles. Dida is always waiting for her. Lotus would like to bring her to live in Dhaka with her, yet she cannot leave her property in the village.

Lotus gets up from her chair. She remembers that she has to go to the grocery store to buy bread and onions. She went grocery shopping last Thursday but forgot to buy the onions, and she cannot imagine frying eggs, something she eats almost every day, without onions.

She changes from her housecoat and puts on *salwar-kameez*, a traditional dress comprised of a long loose tunic and pants. Lotus wears jeans and a T-shirts usually for casual outings, but when she goes out shopping or to work, she is in her *salwar-kameez*. She decides to go to Meena Bazar. Both the grocery shops, Nandan and Meena Bazar, are close by, but she feels more at home in Meena Bazar.

It is the end of the month, and her wallet is almost empty. The money she had collected from the bank for the month's paycheck is almost gone. Her father had built a two-story house in Mirpur before he left for the United States. It is now rented to tenants and with the income Lotus pays for groceries and an assortment of other expenditures for Dida. However, she makes sure that she saves a small amount every month in hopes that one day she will be able to afford a master's degree from the United States of America. Before stepping out Lotus counts her cash carefully, speculating on how much more she will need for the rest of the month.

twenty-two

As usual, Sunday finds Lotus at her office, ready to put forth her best self. Working in the bank and dealing with the import-export branch is no easy job. It is especially tough because of the long office hours. Still, Lotus, being single, finds enough time to relax during her weekends. By Sunday she is quite cheerful and full of energy. The first client of the day is Adam Islam, a businessman. He has started coming recently and has pleasant manners. Tall and blue eyed, on the first day he had caught Lotus staring at him. He had given a short laugh and said,

"Madam, don't worry I am not an alien with my blue eyes. I'm used to people looking at them, making sure that I am a human. My import permit is legal and your bank is safe with the loans I applied for."

Taken off guard with his bluntness Lotus said, "Oh, I'm sorry. I didn't mean to stare. It's just that blue eyes are not seen so often around here."

Lotus treats him to a cup of tea while she deals with his papers. She gets some tea for herself and gets busy with the other work. Her colleague sitting in the next desk over, Saima, is a busy mother of two small children. Quite often she complains of chores at home keeping her busy with work on weekends too. She often says that Lotus is just fine by herself, and that she should take more time before settling down to a family. Saima's usual comment on getting married goes something like this: "You know, this marriage thing is like a colorful balloon. It is so attractive from the outside, and yet when it bursts strange thoughts are let loose like mysterious gasses. You keep wondering what is wrong and what is right. Keeping a happy marriage is really a challenge these days with both parents working."

Lotus is almost to her twenty-sixth birthday. Her biological clock is ticking. But whenever Saima talks like this, she reminds herself that maybe she can give herself two or three years more before seriously considering marriage. Of course, whenever she thinks of marriage, she remembers Bijoy and falls back into her reveries.

"For the life of me, I wish I could wipe you out of my memories, Bijoy." Lotus often curses under her breath.

Dancing Light intervenes and tries to console Lotus. "You'll get over it in time. It's the thought of a missed happiness that brings Bijoy to your heart so often. You've lost your father and take care of a mother who is physically present but emotionally in a dark void. This makes you unhappy deep down in your heart and so your past happy days rewind themselves."

But that longing to be happy again is always there. Saima, being an old colleague, has heard of Bijoy. On an impulse Lotus even once told Saima, "If you come across someone you think could be to my liking, please let me know. At times I feel so frustrated and lonely."

The mind has an uncanny habit of strumming old wounds, even when one is busy. And while all these thoughts are running through her, Lotus pauses in her work and looks up from her files to find Saima gazing at her intently.

Saima smiles and says softly, "You look up in the clouds, but I think you are coming down to Earth now!" Then she gives a sweet, saucy smile and says, "Lotus, have you noted that young man, Adam Islam, the one with the import business, has been visiting your desk every time he comes in the bank?"

"What rubbish!" Lotus exclaims. "Wait, Adam Islam with the strange blue eyes and tanned complexion? Oh yes, it's just that he happens to have dealings with my department, that is all. No strings attached."

"Don't mind me, but I notice that he takes more than the required time when he is talking to you. And you know he stares at you intensely."

Lotus laughs and says, "Nonsense. It seems as if you are trying to concoct a romantic story for me."

Saima is serious and tries to convince her. "Anyway, he is never in a hurry to leave the seat while he deals with his business. And he takes hours to drink the only cup of coffee he gets from you. You know what I mean? Lotus, I am sure he would love to have second and third cups of coffee if you were to offer."

Lotus bursts out laughing at the vision of her offering cup after cup of coffee to a client and says firmly, "Sorry, Saima, I don't think you are sniffing for romance in the right place."

Saima stops clicking away on her keyboard and says, "I have a sixth sense for smelling out romance. Let's see what comes! He seems to be of the perfect age too, must be around thirty. You know in our country we prefer a bit of age gap."

It is already late in the afternoon, and Lotus wants to finish the day's invoices and let Saima be the winner of the imagined romance. She hates leaving pending work and the mess it makes on the following day.

It is almost seven in the evening when Lotus finally stops working and starts to pack for home. Saima has left long before. She works frantically from the early hours so that she can go home and give time to her children. Her husband, a businessman, comes home much later, and she is the one to help the children with homework and, of course, cook the family meal. In Bangladesh few men think of entering the kitchen to help their wives, and Saima is not one of the lucky ones.

The next day, Lotus finishes her work a little early and is at her mother's hospital, Peaceful Heart. She has been missing her mother, though she has little hope left that Daisy will ever recognize her. But today is a special day. It's Daisy's birthday.

Lotus has not been able to visit the small hospital for the past two weeks, even though it is not far from her office, because she has been feeling too worked up after office hours. Lotus brings a bouquet of orchids for her mother.

It had been Dancing Light who had whispered to her, "Take the orchids. She likes those special flowers."

Lotus listens to the soul's message in her heart and travels an hour out of her way to find the orchids. She has not had the chance to ever learn the likes or dislikes of her mother, but Daisy's soul keeps in close touch with Dancing Light, so there is always something guiding and connecting her to her mother.

As she enters her mother's room, Daisy looks up from the book she is pretending to read. She is always doing that. *Maybe,* Lotus thinks, *she was a bookworm at one point in her life.* Nevertheless, she asks, "How is the book, Mom? I will get some new ones for you next time I come. Look, do you like the flowers? It's your birthday, Ma. Happy birthday!" She holds out the bouquet to her mother.

A sudden flicker of light flashes over Daisy's sad face, and for a second it is as if she were back to her old life. Happiness floods Lotus's heart as Daisy takes the flowers and looks at them for a while. But the momentary light passes just as quickly as it came, and she drops the flowers on the floor.

As Lotus tries to move forward for a hug, Daisy backs away. She settles in her chair, as if to say she is done with her, and takes up her book again. For the past years in the hospital, she has been holding a book in her hands. If the book is taken from her, she reacts violently.

Lotus is her only child, and yet it is this very child she seems to believe is an intruder. Now she is looking at her daughter with annoyance. Finally, as Lotus expects, Daisy puts her book down, comes forward with long purposeful strides, and tries to push Lotus out of the door.

"Ma, I have come to see you," Lotus says while attempting to smile and keep her ground, despite the thin fingers trying to push her away. Feeling turmoil in her heart and working to hold back her tears, Daisy puts her arms around her mother.

Now the mother looks at the beautiful young lady blankly, as if to say, "Who are you? Why are you bothering me?"

Daisy's soul reaches out to Dancing Light and says, "No use. The mind, heart, and I cannot work on Daisy's depression. She will not come out of her hell. She is a captive of her mind. There she is still with Tareq, and she can't find him anywhere here. When Lotus comes, she longs to see him. The girl reminds her of the love of her life. I am trying to work through this mindset. It's a war between her physical self and my invisible being. Only the Creator knows who will win."

Lotus steps back and stands aside, looking at the frail figure of her mother. Her hair has grown white and her body seems to have shrunk, her eyes hollowed. The wide mouth is set in a firm line, as if guarding the gates of her inner world. Her eyes carry the haunted look of years of loneliness and dozens of medications.

On rare days, Daisy smiles at her daughter and does not try to drive her away from the room. But this is not one of those lucky days, and Lotus feels very sad. She decides to leave.

"Ma, I am going now. Please, make sure that you eat well," she says to her mother, remembering the doctor's complaint. Her mother has become much thinner as of late. Before leaving the hospital, she talks to the doctor on duty to inquire about Daisy's health and to see if she requires anything.

The doctor informs Lotus that her mother has consented to watching television once in the last week, and that seems to point to some improvement. As Lotus passes through the hospital gate, she prays for more good news on her next visit.

twenty-three

On her way home, Lotus decides to have a look around Rapa Plaza, her favorite shopping mall. She has two hours to browse around before the shops close. Maybe she can find a nice hairclip or a pretty shade of lipstick. It is the end of the month, and she is not planning on any big spending, but even window-shopping is fun. In fact, window-shopping is much more her style, as she does not like overspending or buying things she does not need. Her wardrobe is very limited, just clothes she really needs for her office and occasional outings. But this does not keep her from feeling content with life. A simple life is her code of happiness.

Lotus checks the prices of the few dresses that catch her fancy. They are quite expensive, and she decides that she would rather buy her own materials and make the dresses at a cheaper price. Lotus has learned to tailor most of her own clothes, for Dida always encouraged her to sew and save money.

As she is just about to take out a handbag that looks rather nice, she hears a male voice beside her say, "Hello! What a wonderful surprise. I did not expect to meet you outside your office, madam!"

Lotus turns to find Adam Islam, her bank client, standing beside her. Immediately, Saima's tale of how he lingers around her desk comes to mind, and she is at a loss as to what to say to the gentleman. After all, she has only ever discussed business with him up to now.

She manages to stutter, "Oh, hello! I did not expect to meet you here either."

Lotus finds herself looking closely at Adam. She thinks that he has a certain Greek look about him. His fair complexion has a light tan, he is tall and muscular, and his dark hair gives him a little something exotic. His lovely blue eyes make her sure he is linked to a Western ancestor.

Lotus pauses to smile at Adam and then continues quickly, as if glad to find something to say. "This is my favorite shopping complex. Whenever I have time, I just drop in to have a look around."

"That is surprising," Adam says. "In fact I too come here on and off. I buy toys for my son here. He just turned five. And Hollywood, the CD shop, is my favorite place for checking out movies and music."

Lotus looks down to see that he is holding a toy car in his hand. The mention of a son seems to settle Lotus's nerves. *So, this man is married and a father too. Then why did he try to find an opening with me? Am I just being imaginative along with Saima?* Her imagination running ahead of her, she puts up a defensive shield. *Is he looking for an extramarital affair, a distraction from an unhappy marriage, perhaps?*

Adam is looking at her handbag and remarks, "I see you have picked up something. Are you going to buy it?"

"Yes, it looks different, and I was thinking of taking it," Lotus says, still looking at the bag in her hand. Suddenly, before Lotus has time to register what is happening Adam snatches the bag from her and gives her a disarming grin.

He holds the bag tightly and says, "Madam, if you don't want an official complaint for insulting a client, allow me to buy this bag for you as a gift for talking to me amid these hundreds of shoppers." Adam moves his hands in a dramatic gesture, pointing to the people around them. Then, giving her a mischievous grin that seems to speak of his pulling her legs, he says, "I am happy that you did not turn your face away and pretend not to know me."

Lotus bursts out laughing. "Oh dear, do I look so snobbish? Why in the world would I turn my face away from a person I know?"

Adam gives a short laugh, saying, "That is a relief! You make my day." He then quickly turns to the counter to pay for the bag and has it wrapped with gift paper by the sales personnel. He holds it out to Lotus, "Please, do me the honor of accepting this humble gift, but be sure that I treasure our fated meeting much more than this measly gift can show."

Lotus is taken aback. *Is Adam always as impulsive as this?* But she manages to say, "Why would you buy this for me? I only do my job at the bank. I never do anything out of my way for you."

"It is my privilege, madam, to be able to give you such a small gift." Adam is smiling at her. "Please, just take it as a gift from a new friend. I promise I will not ask you to give me illegal import permits."

Lotus cannot help laughing. Looking up at his eyes, she catches her breath. It is as if they are looking into each other's souls; there is a familiarity there, as if they have known each other for ages!

Adam gives another of his magical smiles. "You don't have to be scared of me. You have all my contact information. In case I rob you of your heart, you can call the police on me."

Lotus is astounded at the boldness of his jokes. She doesn't know how long she has been looking into those deep eyes, but something gives way within her, and she suddenly trusts this person she has only ever known before as a client. In a fraction of an instant, he is no longer just a client, but like an old friend, someone she knows she can trust.

Lotus looks at the tall man in front of her. Is he crazy, or is she the crazy one to be feeling like this? Why is he making such advances if he is married? But looking at his charming smile and handsome manly face, she is compelled to give him the benefit of the doubt. She does not feel like hurting this friendly person. Maybe he does want to just be friends. These days, men and women do become friends without it turning into romance.

While these thoughts race across her mind, Lotus smiles at him. She makes up her mind. Suddenly she is not afraid of Adam and rather feels curious about him and his life. At this moment the fact that he is married simply does not matter to her. *What's wrong with a friendship?* Somewhere bells seem to ring, bells that tell her to be free and happy with this happy-go-lucky young man.

At that moment Adam's soul transmits to Dancing Light, "Hello, there. Adam's mother is American. Finally you have got her feeling something for a man other than Bijoy. I too have been working on Adam to bring on these warm feelings for Lotus. Let's hope our plan takes us somewhere. The brain and the reasoning self are interfering brats. They don't want to place passion above reason."

Lotus looks at the handbag for a while. Somehow the bag now holds special meaning for her. She looks into Adam's eyes. She can see hope written in them, and at the same time she can see fear, the fear of rejection. She will not hurt this being who is trying to be a friend.

"I like the bag very much. Thank you. You did not need to buy it for me, but I will take it," Lotus says as Adam hands her the package along with the receipt. She smiles at him, saying, "Do you live near? You were saying you come to this shopping mall often." Lotus then adds, "I live right down this road, which is one of the reasons I come here from time to time."

"I don't live near exactly, but my house is not far from here either," Adam says as he puts his wallet in his pocket.

Lotus notices that he is meticulously dressed in pressed trousers, a crisp blue long-sleeved shirt, and newly shined shoes. He is a perfect gentleman in both looks and manners. Adam reminds her of the young men she met when in the United States. It has been a long time since she has had an instant liking for a man. But at the back of her mind, an alarm goes off and she reminds herself that he is married and has a son.

Looking into his blue eyes and at his fair complexion, she is unable to suppress her curiosity. "Do you mind if I ask you a question? You seem to have some foreign traits in your features. Are you full Bangladeshi? I am an American. Well, Mom is American, and my father was a Bangladeshi American. He died before I was born in a car crash. I grew up with my grandmother here."

Adam is grinning down at her as they walk side by side, walking toward the exit of the mall. In fact he is looking deeply into her eyes as he says, "See, it's our ties to the past that have brought us together. My father is an American, and my Mom is a Bangladeshi. They met and married when Mom went to get her master's degree at UT Austin. But unfortunately, the marriage lasted for only five years. Dad got involved with a Southern belle and then married her. Suddenly he was all into being American and found the new lady more fitting. I suppose that is one of the cultural issues that arise on occasions in cross marriages."

He pauses and holds the door for Lotus as she exits onto the street before continuing. "Anyway, Mom came back home and joined a private university as a lecturer. I am an American by birth."

Dancing Light feels a flutter inside her. Unknown to her, it is Adam's soul nudging her.

"Dancing Light, we have to get busy, work on their chemistry."

Dancing Light immediately has the heart and the brain to work out the chemistry for Lotus to feel something for this young man.

Adam's soul reaches out, saying, "You see how we met so far away from our native soil? Do you think that means these two will connect and find romance?"

"But Adam speaks of a son. How is he single? Where is his wife?" Dancing Light asks.

Adam's soul sighs. "Let us keep that for now. But he is single at the moment, so work on your host to make them connect."

Taking the advice, Dancing Light gets busy keeping Lotus feeling curious and making her feel warmth seep into her heart as she crosses the street with Adam. Dancing Light says to Adam's soul, "I can hardly wait until Lotus falls in love again. But you know that her brain at times is afraid of new relationships. She shuts me down whenever I try to make her feel butterflies for someone. How about it, this time you and I together will try to win over their minds and make these two fall in love."

Adam's soul is excited and sends the tremors of love to his host so that Adam's heart feels a longing for Lotus. At last his host is going to fall for someone. He says, "Okay, let us make this happen."

Lotus feels elated as Adam talks about his work and hobbies, and something sparks between them. Dancing Light is excited.

"Aha!" Daisy's soul snorts. "I am sure the Creator has plans for these two. He is bringing them together for a reason."

As if by silent consent, Lotus and Adam start to walk on the pavement together in unison. After a while Lotus looks around and says, "I have to call a rickshaw. So I will walk on and be on my way. Thanks for the bag."

To say good-bye, she holds out her hand in a friendly gesture. Adam takes it gently, but instead of saying good-bye, he says, "Madam, if you do not take offense, I have a humble car, and I would be more than happy to drop you off. May I have the honor?"

As Adam stands close by her side, Lotus smells whiffs of his cologne. And she likes it. Somehow it seems to draw her closer, and she feels a tug in her heart.

Lotus looks at his face. The manly face with serious eyes looks down at her intently, as if afraid of being refused. Lotus smiles up at him and replies, "Well, if it is no trouble for you, I would love a ride. The sky is dark, and it might start raining at any moment."

As Lotus gets into Adam's car, a feeling of familiarity floods her. It is almost as if she has been in this car many times before. The car feels familiar and comforting.

"Thanks!" she says as Adam holds the door for her.

Somehow Adam, his car, his smell, all have brought on a sense of déjà vu. Lotus cannot make heads or tails out of her feelings, and sighing she settles down in her seat. She watches Adam's hands with their slim fingers holding the steering wheel. It is weird, but she is sure she can feel Tareq smiling at them, as if her father is happy for her.

On this fateful day of Adam and Lotus's meeting, Dancing Light suddenly is aware that a spirit is hovering nearby, and she knows that it is Tareq's. He has come on a momentary visit to his daughter but cannot stay. She just barely makes out his voice echoing in space. "I am making sure that Lotus is receiving this transmission from her father's soul," says the spirit. "A father's soul does not desert the child he fathered on Earth. Even after death the soul sends signals of approval. A father and mother's love for their children has no limits. The souls cannot come back to the human world after a person dies and so we, the spirits, come on their behalf."

Dancing Light replies, "I can well imagine it. When we souls time travel, often our hosts are asleep in the deepest levels, and then we get a glimpse of how the beloved departed souls have loved the living ones."

Tareq's spirit flutters around, knowing well that he will be pulled back at any moment but still wanting to be near his daughter. He continues, "This love between humans, blood ties and romance, is the essence of life that the Creator gives. I have met so many other spirits that go down to Earth to console hearts broken in betrayals of love. Some even take their own lives when romance fails. Men and women end up hating each other. These are times when passion rules over hearts and physical intimacy makes souls suffocate or dance as you feel the pains or the pleasures. The Creator indeed has strange ways of playing with this human race."

Wide-eyed, Dancing Light listens. Lotus is not deep into sexual desires, but all of that comes in the package with romance. This is a new lesson for her Dancing Light, so she asks, "I witnessed Tareq and Daisy having sex when Lotus was put inside her mother's womb. But I had no idea that the world beats drums about it. But I suppose, without sex, children will not come, and the human race will end."

"Yes, coupling is necessary for reproduction." The spirit explains. "Mating exists in some form with every living thing, but this tremendous force of love between the sexes is perplexing.

These days there are those of the same sex getting married or living together. I personally think these humans give sex too much weight in their lives. Some things are more attractive when taken privately. But no, they go berserk about it…sex…sex…the physical, the mental, and the battle of the sexes in the working world."

"Wait," says Tareq's spirit as he talks and watches Lotus and Adam in the car. "Dancing Light, put your host at ease, ask Adam's soul to do the same, and make sure they have a next date."

Leaving the souls to do their jobs, Tareq's spirit disappears. Dancing Light knows that the Creator has taken him back, maybe to send him to another corner of the world. Spirits, as far as she knows, are sent in different forms, sometimes even in the forms of other animals. She wonders where this spirit is going to and for what. But she slows down her curiosity. Souls are supposed to be passive beings, not curious and restless like the hearts and the minds that often drive their hosts crazy.

twenty-four

Meeting Adam has left Lotus thunderstruck. All of a sudden, things seem to be changing, and her thoughts are constantly rewinding to her evening with the young man. It is twilight now, and Lotus has just come back from her office. Chaiti is in her room, typing away on her laptop. Chaiti loves her job as a journalist. She is a bookworm, who loves to write fiction and poetry. From time to time, she shows Lotus her publications in local newspapers. In fact, Chaiti has confided to Lotus that she is trying to write a novel. That's why, when she is not in the mood for chatting, Chaiti can always be found clicking away on the keyboard, absorbed in her writing. Seeing that she is quiet, Lotus assumes that she must be working on her novel and wonders what the story is about. Chaiti says it is a secret, and that only on the day it is published will she hand it over to Lotus to read for herself.

Watching the local TV news with the sound turned low, Lotus hears her mobile phone ringing. Rising from the couch on which she is relaxing, she answers the phone. She almost topples over a table upon hearing the caller's name. It is Adam calling her. *Where did he get my phone number? Oh, of course, my business card has the office number, and I gave him my card on the very first day he came to the bank.* She feels her legs wobbling beneath her for with a jolt she understands that there was a twist. Fate seemed to have intervened and she had by mistake given her personal visiting card to him instead of the official one that day. That one had her personal contact information along with the official one. And he kept it. That must mean that he had always planned to call her someday.

She tries to calm her voice as she asks politely, "How are you? And how is your son? Did he like the toy you bought him that day?"

"I suppose he is all right. You see he lives with my mother. I live alone in my flat."

Lotus is feeling confused. He has a son; evidently he is married. Then why is he living alone? She decides not to pry into his private life and instead says, "Does your son go to school? By the way, what's his name?"

Adam laughs softly. He seems to be glad that Lotus is asking about his son. "My son's name is Zuhan, Zuhan Islam." He pauses and then says, "I call him Zuhu for short. You can call him Zuhu too. That is when you meet him."

Adam is surprised at himself as he says this. After all, Lotus has not mentioned that she wants to meet Zuhan. He tries to cover his slight embarrassment by clearing his throat.

On the other end of the line, Lotus is surprised that Adam wants her to meet his son. Despite her confusion, his mention of having Zuhan meet her seems natural. Lotus finds it extremely easy to talk with him. He talks to her as if she has been a part of his life for ages, as if she were a close friend he trusts.

"Yes, I will call him Zuhu," Lotus says. She wonders when she will see Adam next. Surprised that she wants to meet him as soon as possible, she hesitates before adding, "Umm, I mean that is when we next meet."

Adam gives a short but happy laugh, and before saying his good-bye, he promises, "I will ring you soon. We could go to some place together, you, Zuhan, and I."

Lotus can barely contain her curiosity about his wife. It is a black cloud hanging over her perfectly sunny day. She almost feels guilty, as if she is treading in someone else's territory. But deep down, she trusts Adam and hopes he is not doing anything wrong. Still deeper down, she wants to see Adam again, wants to sit down and hear him talking with his ease and charm. After their good-byes and a promise that she will meet him soon, she places her mobile back in its place on her bedside table.

"But I will try to find out about his wife. I don't want to break up a family," she whispers to herself.

Ever since Lotus was a little girl, Dancing Light has been instilling in her a sense of right and wrong. And as Lotus is worrying about cheating with someone else's husband, Dancing Light feels happy. She is confident that Lotus would never purposely wrong someone. She is leading Lotus as she herself has been directed by the Creator. The souls of wrongdoers never find peace in the world—even after death.

twenty-five

Adam and Lotus are together the next day, sharing dinner. Adam does not bring Zuhan, however, as the boy has school the next day and needs to go to sleep early. They are sitting in a restaurant named Broccoli, a cozy local place. Both have agreed to dine on Indian food. Adam has asked Lotus to go through the menu and choose for them. He says that he is fond of both Indian and Chinese food, and that whatever she orders will be okay with him. They order a plate of appetizers. To suit them both, they choose a plate of cashew salad and a plate of fried chicken wings. Lotus is feeling a little shy, for things seem to be happening very fast.

Adam, a mind reader it seems, is to the point and says, "Food must be according to one's own choice. And I am not shy about enjoying a good meal. Enjoy it with me. This is a blessing to be together, laughing, talking, and eating. I am fed up with lonely dinners."

"Thank you for your thoughtfulness, Adam. I'm sure we should enjoy the time we are sharing," Lotus says softly.

The last time she went out with a man was when Bijoy had been in her life. So outwardly she appears calm and poised, but her inner self is still battling over her feelings about meeting Adam when she knows that he has a wife and a child. *If it turns out that he is cheating on his wife, I will walk out of his life*, she promises herself. However, the desire to get to know Adam without judgment is important to her before she risks pushing him away.

In a way, her emotions are ruling over her reason, but how could they not when she is facing Adam and loving every moment of being in his company. In the back of her mind, she knows she will find out the truth before anything becomes serious.

As they munch on fried chicken wings, Lotus is aware that Adam is looking at her very intently. When she raises her eyes to his, he seems to read her questioning look and clears his throat. "Umm…there is something that needs to be clear, I think," he says.

Lotus smiles at his hesitancy and asks, "You want to say something to me?"

"I know you are wondering about my wife, given that I have a son." Here he pauses before continuing. "I must thank you for not prying into my life, and for trusting me enough to come out with me."

It is Lotus's turn to feel uneasy as he stops. She wonders what he is going to reveal. There is apprehension written in her voice as she smiles and replies, "I just honored your request and have come today. I'm sure there's a reason for your silence about your child's mother. But be sure, I will not be seeing you if you are betraying her."

Adam is a bit surprised at how firm Lotus is on the topic, as she seems to be so soft in nature. "You see…." He stops again, as if going on is difficult for him. Then looking rather helpless, he says, "You see, we are divorced. Ruby, that is my wife, fell for someone when Zuhan was only two years old and she married again. Evidently she knew the man before she married me. Our marriage was an arranged one. I wonder why people play with serious commitments like a marriage. Why did she marry me in the first place?" He pauses and sighs, saying, "Phew, I have cleared myself."

He is relieved to have confessed and gives a short laugh. He is finally doing the right thing by telling her where he stands regarding his wife. Now the choice of whether or not to continue their relationship is up to Lotus.

Now it is Lotus's turn to keep her face composed and smile back at him. She manages to keep her face calm, but inside she is flying with gratitude. She is so glad that he is single. She looks at him straight in the eyes and holds his gaze for a moment. She feels that she has to assure him that she appreciates his honesty. "I am glad you told me the truth. You see I was starting to feel guilty in case your wife was waiting for you while you are here with me." She pauses and adds, "I didn't want you to get into trouble on account of me."

Lotus tells Adam about Bijoy and how he broke up with her when she refused to marry him. They both feel free after their confessions. Bubbling with happiness, spilling over all they want to share, they talk like small children, one starting on before the other is done.

From the first day he met Lotus, Adam has felt a closeness to her. Somehow he too feels as if he has known her from a long time back. And now with his secret out, he is glad he can see her more, providing the feelings are mutual. He decides to try his luck. "Friday is just a day away," Adam says, smiling. "We could go away to some place nearby and spend the day. Or have dinner in a quiet place?"

Lotus does not want to spend the whole day with Adam, not just yet. Like a wounded animal she wants to tread the world of romance carefully now. She is not prepared for more heartbreak when she is not fully healed from the last one. However, she doesn't want to hurt him either. And so she says, "A quiet dinner would be nice on Thursday. You see, this weekend I am going to our village, because I've promised to see my Grandmother. I call her Dida, by the way."

Adam asks her about her mother. Lotus tells him about Daisy and her hospitalization after her father's death. Tears glisten in her eyes as she tells him of how she has never known a father.

Adam does not hesitate to put his hand gently over hers as it rests on the table. He says simply and truthfully, "I am sorry. But I will be here for you."

The promise is simple, and yet Lotus knows that it is true. She does not pull back her hand and instead gives his a gentle squeeze. The rush of feelings seems to come over them so mutually that both act as though they hold hands every day, though in reality it is the first time they have touched each other. Both know that they like the feel of the other's flesh against their own, and both want more.

Adam's soul is calling out to Dancing Light. "Hey, we need to give them more spark so that the physical attraction grows too. You know, for a real relationship to grow, love and lust must climb the ladder together. But love has to be stronger. Lust alone does not hold on. Passion wears out, but the heart strings sing on."

Lotus is speaking softly and goes on, "Since my father died, I have to support Mom's hospital expenditures and help Dida run the village home. It can be very hard sometimes."

Adam is quiet as Lotus speaks about her home. He wonders how this young lady manages to do it all on her own: pursue a full-time banking career, look after her ailing mother, and run the village home. His respect for her grows with every moment. He realizes that he is growing to like her more and more as he gets to know her, and he can't help but wonder if he is falling in love with her. Maybe it is too soon to think about love, but he has to admit that his feelings for her are powerful. Keeping his thoughts to himself, he looks at his watch. He has to pick up Zuhan from his mother's soon.

Noting that Adam is checking the time, Lotus also realizes that she has to go home. The evening has been wonderful; she is finally enjoying herself after such a long time. She just doesn't feel like going home. She feels a little shy when she realizes that she likes being with Adam.

"Let's go," she says quietly. Knowing well that Adam will drop her at home, she says nothing about finding a taxi. In fact, she is looking forward to the ride with him.

As they climb into Adam's car, he says mischievously, "Ah, this is my opportunity to steal the princess and flee to the mountains. It's dark and nobody will see."

Finally finding herself comfortable with his flirting, Lotus flirts back. "Don't worry, you won't have to steal the princess. She would be glad to go to the mountains with you."

Adam gives her his most brilliant smile and replies, "Thank you for such trust. Now I know my place is beside you."

His left hand reaches out and touches her folded hands on her lap for a fraction of a moment before going back to the steering. Lotus gasps with his gentleness, and she can tell that he wants to hold on. And so does she.

There is a wonderful smell of fresh lime inside the car. She wonders at the coincidence that Adam also uses fresh lime fragrance. She is always spraying her room with the same scent.

Sitting close to him, she gets a whiff of the familiar cologne. She had loved it the first time she smelled it. Suddenly she wants to have his fragrance surrounding her all the time. She feels as if she is not alone anymore, as if Adam is standing by her in this huge world.

Adam is thinking that he likes having Lotus beside him as he drives. Suddenly he wishes that they could go for a long drive somewhere together.

As they near Lotus's apartment, he says, "You know, Lotus, I hate to see you go. I was so happy being with you."

For Lotus this confession seems to open a floodgate of emotion, and she says, "Same with me. I too feel like staying with you. Somehow it's so good and easy being with you."

In front of Lotus's home, as she is about to step from the car, Adam holds out both his hands to her. Lotus clasps them in hers. Adam holds her hands as if he does not want to let go of her.

With Dancing Light and Adam's soul busy sparking the flames of love, Adam and Lotus are feeling the warmth with every touch. Lotus presses his hands for a second before she gets out of the car. On a sudden impulse, she asks, "Would you like to come in for a second, to see my place?"

The words are out before she even has time to think twice. Adam does not hesitate and replies, "Why not? Since we have become friends, I would love to come inside. Not only that, but one day you must come to see my place as well."

Inside Lotus's apartment she offers him coffee. Adam declines. He does not want her to go to the bother. He asks, "Will your roommate not mind my coming in?" He is feeling a little uneasy. He has never visited a home shared exclusively by females. Ever since Ruby left him, he has not been close to any woman.

"Not a bit," replies Lotus. "We trust each other to know who can come up." Opening the gate of the apartment she smiles and welcomes Adam while telling him the name of her roommate. She goes on saying, "She occasionally brings in her boyfriend. She has a steady, you know, and they are planning to get married." Lotus looks at Adam and holds his eyes for a second, hoping that he will not feel uneasy.

Adam stays for a little while. And then, though seemingly reluctant to leave, he says that Zuhan has to be picked up. He stands and holds out his hand again, as if craving just one more touch from her. Lotus holds her own hands out to him, and as they touch they feel a deep yearning to fall into each other's arms. Adam closes his eyes for a moment, as if trying to ease the fire of his emotions. If he is unable to control himself, he is sure that he will do exactly what his whole body yearns to do: take this woman and make her his own. Lotus's hand clings to his, and she too feels unspoken desires pass between them. Suddenly both seem to wake up, and they move away from each other unsteadily.

"I'll be going, Lotus, but we will see each other again." he says, as if to break the moment's heavy magnetism. But nonetheless, his voice is firm with promise.

After Adam leaves, Lotus remembers that this is the first time since Bijoy left that she has been out for a date. She sighs. She hates to admit it, but somewhere deep in her soul she still has soft thoughts for the devil. Yet somehow this time, as she finds a patch of cloud covering her happy thoughts, she is able to blow it away, revealing Adam's face staring down at her, smiling like the sun to warm her through.

On her CD player, she plays a song from Rabindranath Tagore while she gazes at the countless twinkling stars in the night sky. She listens to the words, feeling an inner glow.

Edin aji kon ghorego khule dilo daar? (Which doors has this day opened today?)

Aji prate shurjo utha shofol holo kar (Who has found joy in the sunrise of today?)

Bone bone fhul futeche dole rongin pata (Flowers bloom in the forest and the leaves sway.)

Kar ridoye majhe holo tader mala gatha (Whose hearts are twined into a garland?)

Tagore, the bard of the literary world, known all over the world for his versatile songs, poems, and prose, is Lotus's retreat into her deepest thoughts. Tagore's songs and poems offer her the tears and joy that are her heart's solace.

That night, when Lotus enters the deepest stage of sleep, Dancing Light travels forward in time to see the future of Adam and Lotus. She is intrigued by how powerful love can be, and her host is certainly in love again. It can be heavenly, and it can be catastrophe. But Dancing Light finds her way blocked. It seems the Creator wants to keep this knowledge strictly to himself. Dancing Light just hopes that things turn out well for Lotus.

Lotus is in a new world of romance. Her dreams lead her through mountains and seas. She is a bird flying in the sky with another bird. Together they fly high and low, but she is uncertain if the other bird will be able to fly with her through the endless blue world if she decides she must fly to new heights.

twenty-six

It is the first weekend of the month, and Lotus is in her village home. Dida is very happy to have her beloved granddaughter with her. She proudly looks at Lotus, who seems to be growing prettier every day. Dida chuckles merrily as she asks, "Why is it that you look like a blooming flower? Has some bee come to seek honey from you?" Dida says as she twitches her granddaughter's nose playfully.

Dida had known Bijoy and liked him. When Lotus broke up with him she was disappointed, as she was hoping that Lotus would settle down, get married, and have children after she received her degree. After all, she was going to be twenty-six years old. Although her tall, slender body does not show her age, nevertheless, Dida worries for her only granddaughter.

Lotus is used to Dida cracking jokes about her love life. After all the granddaughter and grandmother relationship is very sweet indeed. Lotus wonders if her feelings for this newfound love are showing on her face. Usually, she does not feel like leaving the village, but this time she is looking forward to going back to Dhaka and seeing Adam again. She recalls the electric shock waves that passed through her when Adam touched her hand. Her heart had wanted him to hold her hands a bit longer, had wanted something more.

It is morning, and Lotus sits with Dida having puffed rice and hot tea. And of course Dida made those special coconut balls for her. They are sitting beneath a tree in the front yard. They rest on low wooden stools that look like footrests. They are silent, just enjoying the bliss of being together.

The village looks beautiful all around, the trees and fields covered in luscious greens. The rainy season is almost over, and the sky is dotted with patches of white clouds. Autumn is showing its face in the white, feathery kans grass flowers. The vast blue sky hangs overhead like a blue canopy.

Dida is cutting her betel nut as she sips her tea. Her hands are seldom idle. It is late in the afternoon, and tomorrow is Saturday. Lotus will be going back to Dhaka by the afternoon's bus. Dida is always unhappy if she takes the early morning bus. Although sometimes it is night by the time Lotus reaches Dhaka, she wants to make Dida happy and so takes the afternoon bus.

Hearing her mobile phone ringing, she hastens inside the house. It is Adam. She had informed him of her coming. Somehow she felt that he would be disappointed if she traveled without letting him know. He is on his way from Zuhan's private teacher, he says over the phone. "I wish you were here. We could have coffee somewhere."

Lotus likes to hear that he misses her. It is good to know that someone thinks of her, and that someone being Adam makes her very happy. She herself has been thinking of him off and on ever since coming to Moinatori. And now Dida's jokes make her think of him all the more. *Maybe*, she thinks, *after some more time, if I get to know Adam better, I will tell Dida about him.* She is sure Dida will be happy. She hopes that one day she will be coming home with Adam, telling Dida, "Here is our new family member, Adam, my husband to be!"

After talking with Adam, Lotus rejoins Dida to finish tea. With the betel nut in her mouth, Dida looks at Lotus long and hard. Indeed the girl looks flushed and happy. She wants to ask more questions about her office and the secretive smiles. She usually asks a question or two about Chaiti and her fiancé, but today she says, "A penny for your thoughts?"

When Lotus does not respond, still looking intently at her granddaughter's preoccupied face, Dida adds, "Make sure your reason and passion are balanced, dear."

Lotus is surprised by her grandmother's intuition, though she knows she shouldn't be. Dida has a sixth sense about her granddaughter and knows something is going on, but she does not want to pry.

Dida knows that her granddaughter would tell her if there had been any profound changes in her life. It is almost noon, and the time for Lotus's departure is at hand. She asks Lotus to have her lunch an hour early so she can be on her way with extra time. The sky is filling with clouds and that worries her. Looking at the sky, she remarks, "See how the weather is changing? It is autumn and rain clouds still fill the sky. Why, in autumn, the sky is supposed to be eternally blue. Weather is crazy these days."

But Lotus is thinking that it might be a good thing to get some rain. After all, the summer has been very dry. *Better late than never*, thinks Lotus. She hurries inside and sits down to her early lunch. Knowing well that Dida won't join her, still she calls out to her. "Won't you join me in eating this delicious fish you have cooked? The arum leaf fry is too good today, Dida!" Lotus says as she takes more of the hot rice Dida has cooked for her.

Dida smiles, saying, "You know my lunch hour is at five. After all, I take rice around ten every morning." Like most of the village people, Dida has hot rice and mashed potato in the morning and eats a late lunch.

Lotus is feeling impatient to be back in Dhaka as she washes her hands after lunch. In the village she resorts to eating with her hands, but in Dhaka these days, it is mostly knives and forks. Most Bangladeshi people cannot enjoy eating rice dishes unless they can scoop up the bites with their fingers. There seems to be a special connection between traditional dishes and the use of hands to eat them. Lotus feels the truth of this connection when she comes home and enjoys Dida's cooking.

Grabbing her things she gets ready to leave. She smiles to herself when she realizes that this impatience has a lot to do with Adam. *I suppose feelings are unpredictable,* she thinks to herself. Sometimes feelings do not change, even over decades, and at times they can change within days. When Dida offers *naru* (coconut balls) to take with her to Dhaka, Lotus accepts eagerly.

She is thinking of serving them to Adam if he visits again. Maybe he will be happy to have something from her village home. After all, they are city dwellers, and these village delicacies may be new offerings for him.

Lotus is humming softly while she lifts her small travel bag onto her shoulder. She puts the coconut balls in a paper bag and smiles, thinking that Dida is an expert at making these sweets. Adam might appreciate the old lady's homemade goodies. Has he not already started asking about Dida? He has said that he would one day like to meet her.

Daydreams catch her off guard as she imagines Adam right in this small cottage, sharing food and laughter with her loved ones. She cannot help but wonder if that may happen soon.

twenty-seven

It is almost nine in the evening by the time Lotus reaches her apartment. Chaiti is at home clicking away on her laptop. Feeling tired from the rickshaw ride from the bus station, Lotus sits beside Chaiti. "How was the day? Did you go out?" she asks her busy roommate.

Chaiti stops writing and puts down the laptop. Taking a deep look at Lotus, she says, "Before I tell you anything, you have to tell me about the young man who came up the other day. Didi, have you found somebody at last?"

"Who told you about him?" asks Lotus, surprised that Adam's visit is already news.

"Why, Lily Auntie was asking me if I knew who came up with you."

"So, Lily Auntie, our non-interfering landlady does bother her head about me," Lotus says in a singsong voice.

Chaiti tells her about the landlady's inquiries and gives a wide smile, as if to make Lotus open up with news of her secret visitor.

Lotus smiles. "Lily Auntie is quite the curious cat. Does she keep her windows open all the time, even at ten at night, to see who is coming to our apartment?" Lotus twitches her lips as she does when she is not sure whether to be annoyed or amused. Then she says, "Having the landlady living in the opposite apartment can be a problem. Why that was the first time Adam came—"

She barely utters the name before Chaiti jumps up, shouting, "Aha! So you call him by his first name. I am sure something is going on. Didi, I'm really happy for you. You need someone to share your life."

Lotus laughs, saying, "Don't get too many ideas. We've just met and happened to have shared some tea and dinner. That is all." She goes on to give a brief account of how she met Adam while she hopes that the warmth of her feelings for him does not show too clearly in her eyes. But Chaiti, being a jolly soul, at once begins begging her to go out to celebrate.

"What to celebrate, Chaiti?" Lotus asks, sounding uncertain. "I haven't made any decisions about him, and I don't even know what Adam thinks of me, really. I'm not sure where we are heading. But I do like him so far."

Chaiti gets up from her chair and hugs Lotus, planting a kiss on her sweet face. She gives Lotus a secretive smile as she says, "Didi, smile! I am sure lots of things are about to happen. Imagine you bringing home a man after all these years. That certainly speaks for itself."

To add spice to Chaiti's blind predictions, the phone rings and it is Adam calling, wanting to know if Lotus arrived safely back in Dhaka. "Are you safe and sound, Lotus? I can hardly imagine young ladies these days journeying alone all the way from village homes."

"You know, life has to be taken in its own stride. Who is going to accompany me every trip I take to see my grandmother? I have to take my own situation and handle it the best I can. By the way, how was your weekend?"

"Okay, but I felt lonely without you," Adam says slowly, as if allowing the words time to take effect.

Lotus can feel the truth of what he is saying in his voice. She feels elated. They talk for a while longer, planning their next weekend together. Chaiti has been listening to the phone conversation and heard Lotus say, "I miss you too!" just before getting off the phone. Lotus finds Chaiti staring at her and pressing her mouth with both hands to keep herself from laughing with excitement. When Lotus slaps Chaiti playfully, they start laughing as if they have just become the keepers of a deep secret. Both can hardly wait to see what will be the final outcome.

The next morning, Chaiti is out even before Lotus awakes. Evidently she has some important meeting or some urgent news story to cover. Lotus hurries through her morning routine getting ready for the office. But despite her best efforts, she is ten minutes late in stepping out. She cannot find the three-wheelers she usually takes to work, but manages to hail a taxicab and settles for that, feeling rather happy that she won't arrive too late. On her way she calls Saima and requests that she cover for her until she reaches the office. Saima is a good soul, and Lotus knows she will try to keep Lotus safe and take care of her clients along with her own.

When Lotus enters the office, Adam is waiting, sitting by her desk. *So he is giving me a surprise! He did not mention anything about coming this morning last night when we talked on the phone,* thinks Lotus.

Saima gives a big wave from her place and points to Adam, flashing a big grin as if to say, "I told you so!" Adam smiles as Lotus settles down, telling him how all the three-wheelers have suddenly vanished.

"You could have just given me a call when you didn't find a rickshaw. I always have my car," Adam says, as if she hurt him by not calling.

Lotus smiles and says, "Don't worry, the rainy days are not over yet, not with monsoon season lingering. Almost every morning it still rains. I will call you to bring me to the office in the morning. But don't get mad when I drag you out of bed."

Adam likes her easygoing manners and the quick smile that lights up her face when she talks with him. Ever since his wife left, he has not looked twice at a woman, but Lotus is different. He remembers the first day he met her at the bank. He found her to be very beautiful, and when she talked to him in her soft voice, he thought of how well-mannered and sweet she was.

Adam does not stay long, knowing that Lotus must have a lot of work on the first morning back after a weekend. He accepts the papers he needs and is gone. Lotus feels happy having seen

Adam unexpectedly. It is as if meeting him is a good omen for her. As usual both of them say good-bye in anticipation of their next meeting.

Adams holds out his hand, and Lotus gives him hers. Though a handshake is very formal and expected in the office environment, Lotus feels shy knowing that Saima must be keeping her eyes wide open, taking in the first and last details of her meeting with Adam.

As soon as Adam is gone, the tinkle of an incoming message comes to her cell phone. Lotus checks it and smiles, reading Saima's message: Hi. How did the handshake feel? It's all in the touch, you know.

twenty-eight

The weekdays run on in their usual hectic routine. It is evening, and both Chaiti and Lotus are at home. Chaiti is happy and in a very talkative mood, because she has just been promoted to the position of magazine editor at her newspaper. Lotus listens as she chatters on her cell phone. Chaiti's long, black hair cascades down her back, and her oval face looks lovely framed by her loose hair.

Lotus sits with her hair tied up in a ponytail, her usual moisturizers rubbed into her beautiful face, ready for bed. They have had an early dinner and are just relaxing. Lotus is absorbed in a magazine and from time to time is talking to Chaiti.

Lotus hums her favorite English song, "Summer Wine," by the Corrs & Bono. "Strawberries, cherries, and an angel's kiss in spring...."

Dancing Light calls out to Daisy's soul and says, "This is called a blood connection between mother and daughter! Why, this was Daisy's favorite song too, and she listened to it all the time after she fell in love with Tareq."

Daisy's soul is in a somber mood and remarks, "Aha, I know. And that would seem to send the message that Adam and Lotus have found each other, right?"

Lotus hears her cell phone ringing. She jumps, thinking it might be Adam. She has not talked to him since the morning. As she looks at the screen, she sees an unknown number.

Shrugging, she picks it up regardless, thinking it could be Adam from a work phone.

"Lotus, will you talk to me?" Bijoy says from the other end of the line. "How are you?"

Lotus's heart screams as she tries to absorb the fact that, after so many years, she is hearing from Bijoy again. She is quiet for a while and then speaks very softly, "How can I help you, Bijoy? Is there anything you need? Is there a reason to remember me after your long disappearance?"

She uses a very formal cool tone, although it is very hard for her to keep her voice steady. In her mind she can see Bijoy's face. *Does he look the same after such a long time? Maybe he has changed. Is he married?* Hundreds of questions run through her mind as she waits for him to say something.

She hears an intake of breath before Bijoy begins speaking again. "Lotus, I have not been in the country. I was away in Malaysia. I was trying out some business ventures there. I have only come back yesterday."

Lotus wants to blurt out, "People can call from Malaysia. You didn't call once all this time." Instead she is very calm and simply says, "Okay. But why are you calling me? I mean, why do you remember me after such a long time, Bijoy? I am sure your life is not an empty shell without me, otherwise you would have called a long time ago." Lotus is aware of the anger in her voice. She hears another sigh travel through the line.

Bijoy is quiet for a while, and then he goes on, "Do you want me to apologize, Lotus? I know I made a mistake by trying to rush you into marriage. But that was a much younger, much more emotional me. Believe me, I have not even seen another woman since leaving Bangladesh. I did not ever forget you or stop loving you."

Lotus feels a soft whoosh of breath escape her, as if someone has hit her in the chest. *What is the use after such a long time?* She is asking herself. *What is the use of beating this old drum?* Although she has missed him immensely, hearing from him seems to only add to the bitterness of the past, and she feels only anger toward him.

She says, "Look, Bijoy, I don't know what to say to you. May I put the phone down? I have to work early in the morning. I don't want to have anything to do with you."

"All right, but, Lotus, I will be in touch." Bijoy's icy voice comes from the other end.

Without another word Lotus cuts off the call. She notices that her hands are shaking. She feels a sudden turmoil twisting inside of her. All those days she has spent thinking of Bijoy, and now that he is back, she feels numb. Her feelings for him are suddenly frozen, as if love and hate have together found a saturation point, and her heart is ready to burst with the incredulity of it all.

Chaiti has stopped working and is looking intently at Lotus. She has overheard Lotus's conversation. Her face shows concern as she looks at Lotus's pale face. She takes Lotus by the shoulders and holds her tight.

"Bad news, Didi? What has happened?" she asks. "That was Bijoy after so many years? Didi, you are upset. I will get you a cup of coffee."

Chaiti rushes to the kitchen as Lotus continues to stare at the ceiling, focusing on the revolving fan, as if the whirling motion holds the answers to the thousands of questions bubbling inside her.

Lotus and Chaiti sit together over coffee talking about Bijoy, about how close they were back then. Lotus admits that at times she feels guilty. After all she had known that Bijoy was impulsive and still dated him and then when he wanted a sudden marriage, she had refused. She still wonders why he was so impatient if he really wanted her in his life. Suppose he'd had problems in his life, wouldn't she have waited for him? Chaiti, outspoken as usual, gives her own verdict before she goes to sleep. "I wouldn't give a penny, Didi, for a deserter like him. Are you a cheap garment that he can put on only when he feels like it? Stop justifying his faults. Forget him, Didi. You move ahead…that Adam, he is the one for you. He is like an angel coming into your life."

At the mention of Adam's name, Lotus seems to wake up suddenly, as if jolted from a nightmare. It is as if talking with Bijoy has been a horrible dream and the mention of Adam is the relief one feels upon waking to find yourself safe in bed. *Indeed, have I not been thinking about Adam a lot lately?* In fact, for the first time in many years, she has been able to get over her feelings for Bijoy.

Chaiti has fallen asleep beside her on the bed. She is snoring gently as sleep catches up to her tired body. Lotus knows exactly how tiring it can be to work in the newspaper office and how demanding it is. Feeling tenderness for the younger girl, she plants a gentle kiss on her forehead and gets up.

Though it is close to midnight, sleep is lost on Lotus. She steps out onto the balcony. She stretches and yawns, as if doing so will trick her body into sleep. She knits her brows, thinking of the early hour at which she has to wake up in order to make it to the office on time. For a long time, she stands in the dark, looking down at the sleeping city. The turmoil of her heart finds some solace in the serenity of the dark world. An owl hoots far away.

Elsewhere, a lonely pedestrian mobile phone is singing away, "*Shokhi, shokhi ami je tomar praner bashi…*" (Friend, friend, I am your heart's flute…)

Mobile culture is so ingrained into life! thinks Lotus. Night guards use cell phones to keep themselves awake, playing Hindi tunes to wash away sleep. Even beggars can be found with cheap mobile phones hanging around their necks, while they often go without meals.

"Whatever, I love this country, even with its endless political chaos, pollution, and all," she says softly, as if whispering to someone beside her. She cannot see it, but at that moment Tareq's spirit stands by her side. Tareq's restless soul in the Land of Illumination has requested that the Creator bring consolation to Lotus as she confronts her confusions over Bijoy and her ripples of love for Adam.

Dancing Light, watching Lotus, becomes aware of the spirit and speaks up. "I am having a hard time convincing her that Bijoy should be forgotten. That brain of hers keeps rewinding to the love that they shared. Help me give some peace in her heart and have her feel love and warmth for Adam."

The spirit is invisible yet holds a tremendous strength, and it vibrates positive waves to Lotus's heart, helping her to be sure of her feelings for Adam. Love is a gift from the Creator, but Lotus also knows that true love often travels very twisted paths. And Tareq's spirit prays to the Creator to help his daughter through this emotional period.

Looking up at the infinite sky, Lotus imagines she sees Adam's smiling face. The gentle wind brings his easygoing voice to her ears, and she wishes she could call him then and there. Dancing Light is elated. Ah, Tareq's spirit has gone but their prayers are answered, and love is already making Lotus's heart sing with tender thoughts for Adam.

Yet somewhere Bijoy's voice breaks in. *What is it with first love?* Lotus wonders. *Why do the memories refuse to go away?* Suddenly she is too sleepy to fight, and going to her bed, she falls into an uneasy sleep.

Lotus spends the rest of the night in uneasy dreams. She is standing in a valley. Upon the two mountains ranges, on two sides of the large valley, stand two men; one is Adam and the other is Bijoy. Both are calling out to her.

"Lotus, Lo…Lotus…Lo…come to me…."

※

As Dancing Light is holding Lotus's life up to Tareq's spirit, she can see the father's face full of anguish at the torments of his daughter's love life. But she only smiles and says, "Hold on. Good things come to those who wait with patience and prayers. Your daughter is strong. Let's see what happens."

twenty-nine

Lotus shuffles through her work at the office, but an ominous feeling has refused to lift ever since Bijoy's sudden call a few days ago. He has called again, but recognizing the number, she did not answer. He has left a message, warning that he would drop by her office one day, and Lotus can't help but be tense, expecting him at any moment. She wonders how she is going to react at the sight of him after so many years.

Toward the afternoon, Lotus is called to the manager's room for a brief update of the week's transactions. As she talks, she can hear alerts signaling incoming text messages. Coming out of the manager's room, she checks the messages. Adam will drop in at the end of the day, the messages say. She hopes she can complete her work before he arrives.

Still looking at the papers in her hand, she reaches her desk and is about to sit down when she becomes conscious of someone sitting opposite from her. She stops dead in her tracks as her eyes settle on Bijoy. He is sitting quietly looking at her, his eyes steady, and a small smile playing on his lips. Now that their eyes meet, he speaks. "Hello, Lotus, how are you?"

Lotus feels like shouting, *How dare you appear after so many years and just ask me how I am doing? You have no right to know how I am!* But knowing that he is expecting an outburst from her, she lowers her voice and quietly says, "I am doing fine."

She tries to sound casual, as if she is dealing with simply another client. She steadies her nerves, reminding herself that she is in an office and must remain composed.

"How may I help you? Do you want to open an account?" she asks, looking directly into his eyes. She wants to make certain that none of the emotion passing within her shows on her face. When she sees Bijoy's face fall in humiliation, she feels pleased to have hurt him. No, she isn't the type to hurt other people, but she cannot help feeling the anger boiling inside her. She wants to hurt him more.

Bijoy looks at her face for a long time, as if trying to sum up her words and the thoughts behind the placid look on her face. Quietly he says, "I know you are angry with me. You have perfect reason to be. But today I have come to apologize, to say that I am not at all proud of what I did to you."

"Look, this is my office, and I want you to respect my space," Lotus reminds him softly but firmly.

Bijoy pulls up his chair, as if trying to get more comfortable. "Please, will you see me after office hours?"

Just then Saima walks over. Saima knows about Bijoy but does not recognize him. Lotus has no intention of introducing him, and just to get him out of the office, she looks at him steadily. Rising from her chair, she says, "Look, I have work. I have to remind you again that this is my office, and I have no intention whatsoever of discussing my personal affairs here."

And with that Lotus is up and asking Saima to accompany her as she walks toward the locker room. Saima is quick to ask her about the visitor, and Lotus tells her that it is her ex-fiancé. Saima is quick to intervene and says, "I will attend to your guest, and you can go elsewhere. If there is any work here, you can do it. Just keep calm, okay?"

Lotus watches as Saima hurries toward her desk. She can see Bijoy through the door of the locker room. As Saima approaches him, she sees him rise and leave the office. He is clever enough to understand that she will not talk to him in the office.

After Lotus finishes her work in the locker room, she rewinds her meeting with Bijoy. It is as if all her blood is rushing to her face. As anger boils inside her, she tries to sort out the feelings she once had for him. She feels bitter that he could have thought she would be so easy to pacify after he had left and found her at his whim.

"I'm not your doormat, you know," she mutters under her breath to vent her anger.

Called by Dancing Light, Adam's soul flies in, and Lotus can almost hear Adam's wistful voice tickling her ears. She resolves then and there that she is not letting Bijoy hurt her again. As she walks back to her desk, she has a vision of Adam sitting in the very chair where Bijoy has just been sitting. Lotus wonders if this is fate's way of telling her that a new man is entering her life. Is it to tell her that she needs to get over her feelings for Bijoy, who was not there when she needed him?

Lotus speeds up her work and feels happy remembering that Adam is coming over after work. She wishes she had put on a nicer dress. It has been a long time since she wanted to look pretty in the eyes of a man.

thirty

It is Friday, and neither Chaiti nor Lotus is going home for the weekend. Ever since Bijoy's visit to her office yesterday, Lotus has been very upset. Chaiti volunteered to stay with her in Dhaka so that she won't be alone. Chaiti wants to be near her, to share her troubled thoughts. After breakfast they take a three-wheeler to the lake at Shere-Bangla Nagar, hoping it will be refreshing for them both. The slow ride on a three-wheeler is in its own way relaxing when you have someone to chatter along with. And having Chaiti there to do the talking, Lotus is only too happy to take the break.

"Don't you wish there were more lakes in Dhaka? We would be able to escape the millions of people and find some peace and quiet," Lotus mumbles softly as they settle down on the concrete beside the lake.

The sight of water is supposed to soothe the soul. Chaiti and Lotus sit watching the lake and the people strolling around it. There are hundreds of people with their children, all having a good time. The children are laughing and running around, as if they are free as birds. It is a happy sight.

There is a gentle wind blowing around the lake that makes the ripples chase each other across the surface of the water. The light from the late afternoon sun reflects off the flowing water and creates a magical effect. The wind touching Lotus and Chaiti seems to wake up sleeping thoughts. Since it is autumn, the sky is filled with floating white clouds. Few wispy kans grass flowers sway from side to side just beside Chaiti. Lotus looks at the flowers and smiles at her friend. It is good to be with someone you care for when the world turns upside down all of a sudden.

Bijoy said that he would be in touch, but he has not been in touch at all. That is strange. Usually he is very stubborn once he puts his mind to something. Suddenly Lotus turns to ask Chaiti, "Do you think he came to my office to see if I would give him another chance and, on seeing me so angry, decided to give up?"

Chaiti squints up her nose in thought and says, "If I know anything about human nature, and I am not sure I do, I don't think he would come back into your life only to leave it again so easily. It's something else that's keeping him. I am sure he will get in touch with you soon."

Lotus smiles at her friend, saying, "Oh, you seem to know him so well. But I hope he is gone for good."

"Does that mean that you are sure about Adam?" asks Chaiti, prying as usual, hope written all over her face.

Lotus looks at Chaiti, shakes her head, and shrugging her shoulders says, "To be honest, I feel differently about Adam, but I am not sure what the future holds."

The sky with its white clouds has a fairy-tale look, as if transplanting them to another time. The trees around the two women create shade from the late afternoon sun, keeping them cool. They stare at the peaceful lake. It is indeed a soothing scene, with the wind swaying the trees and birds flying among the branches and over the lake. Once in a while the birds, mostly crows, fly close to the water, swooping down to pick something up and carry it away.

"Chaiti, what are the birds taking from the water? Look how God has made the game of survival. We can see nothing, but the birds can see the food in the water. I think those kingfishers eat the small fish that float around on the lake's surface."

Chaiti nods her head and looking up the sky, says, "Life is a big puzzle that we never solve, I suppose. A superior force must control everything. Why else would life deliver us such ups and downs?"

Lotus gave Chaiti a gentle nudge on the arm, saying, "Aha, the writer is awake. Here we go on life philosophy. Forget those serious things, Chaiti, at least for the moment. We should just fly on some spicy snacks like *fuchka* and *chotpoti*. Look! I see a vendor over there."

The women amble over to buy the popular Bangladeshi snacks from the vendor, and they sit on rickety wooden chairs in the open air while they wait for the vendor to prepare their food.

The vendor is a witty man and seeing them both wearing jeans and shirts, he says humbly, "I don't know how to address you—is it sister or aunt? Days ago women in *saris* were called aunt and women in *salwar-kameez* were called sister. But now you ladies dress in men's clothes, and we don't know what to call you!"

Lotus, knowing well the Bangladeshi custom of shop hosts giving their customers familial titles, gives him a friendly smile. As she takes the plates of *chotpoti* from him, she replies, "These days, maybe it's easier to call everyone 'madam.' It can be used to address all women."

"What do you say? Is that an English word? Now at seventy years of age, do I have to learn English to run my business?"

Chaiti butts in. "What to do? Times are changing. I am sure the young and old ladies called madam will think highly of you and prefer to eat from your van."

The vendor gives her a big smile, showing his brown teeth stained with betel nut juice. Lotus and Chaiti are just in time to hear him greeting a woman passing by, saying, "Madam, what will you eat today, *fuchka* or *chotpoti*?"

And the customer, a middle-aged woman, stops and orders herself plate of *chotpoti* from the old man. The vendors looks toward Lotus and smiles as if to thank her.

Feeling rather good about their little accomplishment, the two women sit back down at their place beside the running water of the lake. There is a hint of winter in the wind. Lotus thinks, *Winter will soon be here!* She looks forward to the dry sunny days. In Bangladesh winter is the time to move around, for the rains disappear with the advent of the cooler days. She wonders if she will be able to vacation this year, perhaps at Cox's Bazar. Cox's Bazar is a beach located along the Bay of Bengal, and it is considered by many to be the world's longest natural sandy beach. She has not been on vacation for a long time. But maybe she and Chaiti can go together. Lotus turns to Chaiti and says, "Do you think we could take a trip to Cox's Bazar this winter together?"

"That would be wonderful. I suppose we could take Rajiv along as a male escort?"

Lotus looks doubtful and says, "But you and Rajiv, don't you think you would like to be on your own? It wouldn't be good at all to have me trailing along."

Chaiti gives a short laugh. "Oh, Didi, you wouldn't be trailing along. You would be with us. You know I am not possessive about Rajiv. It would be nice, and we could feel safer with a man around." She pauses, gives a sweet laugh, and says, "Aha, I wouldn't be surprised if your Adam came tagging along too. He is crazy about you! That would be a wonderful foursome."

Lotus laughs and says, "It's not like you, Chaiti, to want Adam or Rajiv around. You are so independent."

"Didi, you know that our society is not yet free from its gender problems. Who knows, evil men might take note that we are two women on our own and try something. And you know that female abductions in those remote areas are common."

Just before night sets in, Lotus and Chaiti arrive home feeling pleased with their plans for the Cox's Bazar trip. But happiness can be very short lived at times. When they reach their apartment, the guard at the gate hands them a note from a guest. Lotus looks at the all-too-familiar handwriting. Bijoy was here, it says, and was sorry to miss them. The note ends by stating that he will come again.

Lotus is furious. Where did he get her address, and how dare he visit her without even asking her consent? Just then her mobile rings. It is Bijoy, and the name is like a black storm announcing disaster.

"Lotus, I went to your place hoping to have tea with you. Are you home tomorrow? I will come around six. I'm sure you will be home from the office by then."

Lotus can hardly believe she is hearing him right. He goes on to say that he is sorry that he came by without telling her. As she listens to him, it seems as if Bijoy is pretending that nothing happened between them all those years ago, as if they were back to their old ways when they were dating. Lotus almost hisses through her teeth as she says, "Listen, I have to remind you that you and I do not have a relationship any more. I don't want to hear from you, and I don't to see you either."

"Lotus—"

Lotus closes her mobile phone.

Later that evening, Lotus has trouble falling asleep. Pent up anger seems to be making her restless. Tears cling to her lashes. She is not sure whether these tears come from anger, frustration, or emotional confusion.

"I wish I could seal my heart so his image and name would be unable to sneak in," she whispers into the darkness, talking to the night itself.

Dancing Light is having a hard time keeping Lotus thinking straight. Ah, this creepy "love" thing. It sure makes things complicated, but human hearts and minds thrive or die for it.

Just then Daisy's soul reaches out to her. "Hey, from now on, just keep reminding her about the warmth of Adam's relationship and again love itself will do the magic. You wait and see. It is love and insecure feelings of her decisions that keep Lotus glued to Bijoy, but in time she will be over it all."

Dancing Light becomes busy filtering images of Adam into Lotus's heart. With the flame of love she ignites, Lotus is able to overcome all bitterness over Bijoy. Lotus's soul smiles as her host whispers, "Adam, Adam. Where are you?" And with these sweet thoughts in her mind, Lotus falls into a blissful sleep.

thirty-one

Lotus is at her office and sorting out her day's work when Adam calls. She has missed him the past three or four days, so when she sees his name appear on her mobile, she feels ecstatic.

"Hello?" she answers.

"Am I right in thinking that you are happy to receive my call?"

Lotus sighs contentedly and replies, "You bet I am happy to hear from you. You have not been in touch for a few days."

"I know I have not been in touch. You see, Zuhan had a fever and so I was managing him and my work. I had to leave him with my mother when I went to the office, and then I was back early most days to take him home again. Although he lives with her, when he is sick he wants me all the time. Anyway, how are you, Lotus?"

Lotus feels happiness warm her thoughts as she hears her name spoken with a special softness. Suddenly she wants to see Adam very badly. It is as if the anxiety of meeting Bijoy again has her coiling into the protective shell of Adam. She just wants a way out of this trouble.

Bijoy wants to come back into her life, and she is sure she does not want to go back to that past love. A cracked mirror does not become whole again. At times she wonders if she should have been more tuned to Bijoy's unexpected proposal since she had known him to be quick witted. But the love she remembers is entwined with the pain, and Lotus is unsure of how to move forward with a new life. She has not, up to now, voiced her desire to see Adam so openly to him, but she feels that, more than anything, she wants to be with him now. He seems to make life easy, unlike Bijoy who comes with complications. She just does not want any more problems—she has enough of them—so she asks, "Is it possible for you to meet me for a short time today? I'm feeling sort of lonely." *There*, thinks Lotus, *it is out. Relationships need to be built on honesty, after all.*

Lotus and Adam make plans to meet that evening at their old meeting place, Broccoli, and this time Adam is bringing Zuhan. The prospect of meeting Zuhan excites Lotus. She is happy knowing that Adam cares enough for her to let her meet his son. They certainly seem to be heading toward a destination, though the ways are still known only to the Creator.

While quietly singing to herself, Lotus calls Chaiti. She is thinking of going to Mainatori. Dida called on the mobile and asked her to go. Lotus has not gone to see Dida for the past two weeks, and she knows that it must be making the old lady feel lonely.

"Can you make it, dear, this week? I so want to see you." Dida's cajoling voice is enough to convince Lotus that her grandmother is lonely and depressed, and so Lotus tells her straight away that she will come. She gets through the day's work and is feeling better.

After work, as Lotus approaches Adam's car, she is aware of a little boy looking at her with utmost curiosity from the back seat. "Hello, Zuhan," she says as she opens the back door. She smiles at him. He smiles back but says nothing. Instead of taking her place beside Adam in the front, Lotus sits beside Zuhan and takes his small hands in hers. He has Adam's blue eyes. That somehow makes her happy; it is as if all three share a strange connection to a faraway land.

Lotus touches his soft brown curls and says, "I am Lotus. Your father and I are friends. Would you like to have dinner together?"

This time Zuhan smiles back and, taking a brief look at his father's face, visible in the rearview mirror, replies, "That would be nice. I like Chinese food. Can we have that?"

Lotus is surprised at how clearly he speaks. There is no trace of his tender age in his elocution. But she answers him very seriously, "Of course, Zuhan, it will be as you say. I have come to meet you, and it will be my treat tonight."

"Aunt Lotus has lots of money, Zuhan," Adam teases. "But you can tell her that where bills are concerned, I am the captain. Deal, madam? Or else I don't go."

Lotus acquiesces before transferring to the front seat and settling down beside Adam. She gives him a smile, shaking her head and saying, "Oh, okay. But then I'll treat Zuhan to Gelato ice cream after dinner. Let's go. I am sure we are all hungry."

Adam looks sideways at Lotus before starting the car. He is happy to see that she is carrying the bag he gave her. He notes her beautiful hands with their slender fingers and bare nails. Her serene face carries only a touch of lipstick and eyeliner. He likes her natural look. To him she is a classic beauty. On an impulse, he reaches out to press her hands with his own, as if he needs to feel the warmth of her skin. But just in time, he remembers that Zuhan is sitting behind them.

Adam's soul and Dancing Light nudge each other. "Good job! At least the heart is cooperating with us. Now they are emotionally entangled, just what we need to get them together," says Adam's soul.

Dancing Light looks a bit worried and says, "That weirdo Bijoy's soul has been trying to reach me, trying to convince me that he really means to stay with her. Maybe he does, but you see, broken hearts do not heal. Painful memories are things you can't just wipe away. Physical wounds may heal, but the marks on the heart can't be erased simply because one wishes it! We and the heart are keepers of love and hate, the strongest of human emotions."

Dancing Light and Adam's soul relax, readying themselves to bond Zuhan to Lotus so that the ending to this romance can be happy. Again and again they ask the Creator to bless them with strength.

As they eat and chatter away, it is clear that Zuhan is excited to have Lotus listen to all the stories he has to share about his friends and school. Lotus has Zuhan sitting on one side of her and Adam on the other. The little boy is talking over his tomato soup, smearing his mouth with the thick red food after every bite. Lotus leans over instinctually to wipe his face with her right hand. Beneath the tablecloth, her left hand is held by Adam's as he sits on her left. From time to time she feels him squeeze her hand, play with her fingers, and she does the same with his hand. Both of them love the warmth that radiates through their skins.

thirty-two

Very early on Friday, Lotus sets off for the village. Lotus had asked Chaiti to come with her, and she is glad that her friend agreed. She just doesn't feel like going alone. Chaiti goes to her own home upon reaching their village bus stand. Lotus looks forward to the next few days in the small cottage. Being with Dida is so relaxing, a break from her stressful city life. Dida understands her completely. The small cottage with its tin roof is like heaven to her, holding the memories of her childhood. Though it's a single-room cottage, the coziness and warmth of familiar things make it a place of love for Lotus.

On Friday evening Lotus is with Dida. It is dinnertime, and Dida has made a delicious fried *hilsha* fish and a spicy *shutki*, a dry fish curry, that Lotus is fond of. Lotus comes to sit for dinner after washing her hands, but before taking her place, she gives Dida a long hug. The softness of the woman's body makes Lotus realize that age is creeping up to Dida.

Lotus inhales the smell of the flower scented hair oil and talcum powder Dida uses. It is the scent that Lotus will always associate with Dida. Often when she is sitting in her home in Dhaka, she can imagine this smell surrounding her, and she feels close to the old lady. Lotus sits by the small dining table she recently bought for Dida. Before the purchase they ate on the mat.

"Dida, the sight of your *shutki* is making me ravenous. Let's eat. My love for fresh and dry fish really makes me my father's daughter. Isn't that how the saying goes?" She scrunches up her nose as she tries to recall the exact saying,

"It's *mache bhate Bangali,* right? Meaning rice and fish make a perfect Bangladeshi?"

After a few bites of the delicious food, Lotus starts talking again, casually saying, "Bijoy is back from living in a foreign country and is now poking me to be reunited with him."

Dida looks up from her plate and momentarily her right hand, which is filled with rice, is suspended in the air, her mouth hanging open. She looks long and hard at Lotus. "Well, how arrogant men can be. He leaves when he wants and comes back as he wills."

She proceeds to eat but continues to watch her granddaughter carefully. "You are not thinking of getting back with that betrayer, are you?"

Lotus smiles at her understanding, at the concern she feels. "I have not thought of going back to him, Dida. But the way he is always ringing me and coming to my office, at times I feel sorry for him. After all, human beings do make mistakes and we had known each other for some time. At least I can listen to what he has to say."

Dida goes on eating for a while and then says, "I know you can take care of yourself. But I don't trust that man. And by the way, Chaiti tells me that you are seeing a man by the name of Adam. If your heart finds a new love, don't be afraid of it."

Lotus is astonished. *Imagine Chaiti telling Dida all that!* She is now sure that Chaiti calls Dida to give her news of what is going on in Dhaka. How fast word spreads. No wonder people say that gossip is the fastest media. "That chatterbox, Chaiti!" she blurts out, laughing and thinking of how much Chaiti must have enjoyed letting Dida into this juicy story. "She has to tell you about every man I meet. But I know she wants me to settle down as much as you do."

As they finish their dinner, Lotus goes to get the pot in which Dida keeps her betel leaf. She takes some mango pickle for dessert. As Dida chews her betel nut, they talk about this and that until almost midnight. Dida is very happy to have Lotus at home after two weeks. They talk about Chaiti and how good it is to have her living with Lotus. Lotus tells her about Adam, his son, and his divorce.

But Dida is worried and asks, "Are you sure you want to get involved with a divorced man, especially when he has a son?"

Lotus is thoughtful for a while, and then she says, "I have not made any final decisions. It's just that I like him and he likes me as well. But lately, with Bijoy and his efforts to get back with me, I am feeling confused. I think I have a soft spot for Bijoy, even after all this time. Why else wouldn't I be able to just tell him to go to hell?"

Dida looks at her for some time and then simply says, "Listen to your heart; the path of true love can be hard to find."

As Dida falls asleep, Lotus is aware of owls hooting outside. Somewhere far off foxes are also howling. *Nightlife in the village is rather scary*, she thinks. Living in the safety and comfort of the building in Dhaka is certainly a different experience. It is cooler in the village than the city, and the air already holds hints of the coming winter.

Seeing Dida huddling under the end of her sari, she gets down a light shawl from the clothes shelf. She wraps it around the old lady and gives her a hug. Lotus quietly cleans up the dinner dishes, letting Dida rest after her long day. Soon Lotus is beside her, their arms around each other. She is blissful as she feels sleep closing her eyes.

thirty-three

It is late on Saturday morning, and it is a perfect autumn day. The village with its stretches of green paddy fields and yellow mustard flowers looks picturesque. As usual Lotus will be leaving in the afternoon. The morning mist is still hanging on the horizon far away. As Lotus sits under a tree, her eyes travel to the faraway villages. She can only see their outlines in the foggy morning. The tall coconut and betel nut trees are outlined in blue-gray and stand like resolute soldiers after a night of battle. The grass is wet with dewdrops.

Lotus shuffles out of her slippers and allows her bare feet to sweep over the dew, feeling the delicious wetness. As the sun rises, its rays glisten and sparkle like crystal ornaments across the land.

On her right, the paddy fields have taken on a faintly yellow tone. She knows these crops are ready to be harvested by the color, for her early life in the village has taught her about the harvesting and planting of the crops. *How serene the village is,* she thinks.

Lotus knows that her father used to come to see her grandmother almost every weekend when he was a student studying in Dhaka. He started his career in the city, and yet every weekend he was there, home with his mother. He had wanted to take her to live in the city, but she always declined, saying she felt the city to be suffocating. As Lotus's thoughts run on, she slowly becomes aware of a man standing by her side.

"Lotus, how are you?" It is Abul Uncle, a distant relative of Tareq's. Abul Uncle sits beside Lotus, smiling at her. Abul Uncle is in his fifties and has a salt-and-pepper beard that stretches to his chest.

"Abul Uncle, I was just thinking of going to your house but was afraid I would wake you." Abul Uncle acts as a kind of stand-in for Lotus, taking care of many things on the farm in the village for Dida. She had been meaning to discuss matters of business with him for some time now.

"I wake up early to start the day," says Abul Uncle. "You see, poor people's days begin early; they have to get the seeds before other birds come."

"Aw, come on, uncle. You are far better off than many people up here," exclaims Lotus, knowing well that he is just being humble.

As Abul Uncle settles down beside her, Lotus tells him about some of the problems Dida is having with the workers who look after her crops.

Abul Uncle knits his brows and says, "Don't worry. But why did she not inform me? She is a very independent lady. I will talk with those workers."

"Don't mind Dida. You know how she wants to do everything herself—it is a sort of pride, I suppose." Lotus says, though she respects the old lady's determination to do things independently.

"When are you going back to Dhaka?" Abul Uncle asks before getting up to continue on his way home. Lotus rises with him, telling him of her intention to leave as soon as she can and asking him to keep his eyes on Dida. After all, he is the only relative in the village she has.

Dida is up and busy getting breakfast ready when Lotus returns. The rice pudding soaked in fresh milk is delicious. After breakfast, Dida and Lotus sit sipping hot tea. Lotus wants to start for Dhaka. She has planned to meet Chaiti at the bus station in the morning, but Dida wants to be with her awhile more. And so Lotus calls Chaiti again and arranges to meet her in the late afternoon. That means that by the time they reach Dhaka, it will be dark.

The days have become shorter with winter coming in. Lotus is always anxious to reach Dhaka before dark, but it seems there is a tug-of-war, her wishing to go early and Dida wanting to hold her back. Dida has a worried look on her face, and Lotus knows exactly what is bothering her. Giving her a tight hug, she tells her grandmother, "Don't worry, I will not make any hasty decisions. I'll just see what Bijoy has to say."

She pauses as she picks up her small travel bag. "Don't be afraid of Adam. He may be divorced, but these things do happen. That does not mean he is a bad guy. In fact we click, and even his son seems to like me. I already have a place in my heart for the little boy."

"I know you can make your own decisions, but that does not stop me from worrying," Dida says softly, pulling Lotus into her arms. "Well, my dear, just remember that time is flying by and you have got to think of settling down. I want to see you with your family before I pass away."

Lotus plants a long kiss on Dida's soft, wrinkled cheek, her white hair contrasting with her red betel-nut-stained lips. The old lady's sharp nose speaks for her dignity, and though her eyes are lined with crows' feet, they are still very bright. Lotus always wonders how Dida manages to still not need even reading glasses.

"Dida, don't say these things. They make me sad. You are the only person I have to love and console me. I will settle down when I find the right man. I promise you that."

Good-byes with Dida always linger, and Dida follows her until she arrives on the main path to hail a three-wheeler to take her to the bus station. Even as she waves to Dida, her heart yearns to stay. She remembers her mother in the hospital. She wishes she could bring Daisy to the village and that all three of the women could be united. *Maybe one day Ma will be well enough to come with me to our village home,* Lotus thinks to herself.

thirty-four

It is Monday night, and Lotus is just about to go to bed when her cell phone rings. It is Bijoy. His voice sounds tired, and she can't help but wonder if he is sick. Trying to hide her annoyance at his calling so late at night, she asks, "Why are you calling? I think I made it clear that I have nothing to say to you. Is there something special you want to tell me? I was just about to go to bed. I have work tomorrow."

"I know you have work tomorrow, but I didn't call earlier because your roommate was up and I knew you couldn't talk freely. Lotus, just for once, meet me, I beg of you!"

"You can tell me what you want to say right now, Bijoy. I don't think you have anything to say that needs to be said over a candlelit dinner," Lotus tells him firmly.

There is a short silence before Bijoy speaks again. She can hear pain in his voice as he goes on. "I know you are very angry with me, but that will not put me off, Lotus. I have wronged you, and you have all the reasons in the world to be mad. But just once, please come and meet me. How about tomorrow after work? Can you come to Sea Food, our favorite? We can have dinner together. I will pick you up after work. Give me a chance, Lotus. Even God forgives people for the mistakes they make."

She feels something inside her move when he says that God forgives people. After all, once upon a time she was madly in love with this man. For old time's sake, she can listen to him this once. She sighs. "Okay. Tomorrow I will be ready at seven sharp.

You have to pick me up from the office. But remember, I have to be back as early as possible."

Lotus hears Bijoy give a short, triumphant laugh. He says, "I am in luck today. Thank you, Lotus, for agreeing to go out with me. I will be at your office at seven to pick you up."

As Lotus turns off her light and tries to sleep, she finds her thoughts going back to the years when Bijoy and she dated. She thinks of the days they roamed around the city, happy just to be with each other. They had no plans, no places to be, nothing special to do, and yet the days were filled with significance just because they had been together. The room around her suddenly seems to be alive with old memories, as if it is crowded with the hundreds of pieces of laughter, words, and things they did together. He had always been sort of headstrong but she accepted that with humor.

How often they'd had only puffed rice with chili and onions because neither had enough money for a proper lunch. So many days Bijoy had called her when it was raining and asked her to go out into the wet world. They would get drenched, but they would feel thrilled, a sort of emotional cleansing. The rainy season seems best celebrated through getting wet. How often Lotus had looked long at Bijoy's tall, manly frame and felt an inner turmoil. She had found him physically attractive. And Bijoy? He had often said that she looked like a mermaid in her wet clinging *sari*, a mermaid he wanted to bring into his life forever.

Even as these thoughts run through her, Lotus is surprised at herself for having agreed to meet Bijoy. Indeed she thinks she is an example of the old saying, "Frailty, thy name is woman." She remembers Dida's words of advice about listening to her heart. Indeed would she be destroying a chance of happiness with Adam, a man she knows wants her? Yet she could not forget the intense feelings she and Bijoy shared, feelings that still make her heart beat wildly just because he is here with her again. She remembers a part of Sara Teasdale's poem, "Old Love and New."

Dear things, old things
That my old love said
Ranged themselves reproachfully
Round my bed!
But I cannot heed them
For I seemed to see
Dark eyes of my new love
Fixed on me!

Her thoughts shift to Adam. She has not called him since coming back from the village. She has seen calls from him on her cell phone but has not yet returned them. Somehow she wants to have this meeting with Bijoy done with before she talks to him. But there is a guilty nagging in her mind. Should she not be honest with Adam? Why then is she seeing Bijoy again?

It is almost midnight, and Lotus is just about asleep when her mobile beeps. Sleepily, she checks her phone. It is a message from Adam: "Goodnight and sleep well. Get in touch when you are free." The message is complete with a smiley face and flower emoticon.

"I will be in touch. Are you and Zuhan okay? Sorry I was not in touch," she texts back.

"That's okay. Don't worry."

Lotus's eyes, heavy with sleep, seem to refuse to close as Bijoy's face stands before them. Dancing Light is alarmed. Why does the heart of Lotus melt for Bijoy? She then coerces her host into a very deep sleep and prays to the Creator to help her with a very romantic dream about Adam. The Creator is there, helping out, and Dancing Light can see Lotus dreaming about Adam kissing her.

thirty-five

The next day at the bank, after finally stacking all her files, Lotus picks up her handbag and gets ready to meet Bijoy. She wears a *sari*. She does not want to look like the younger version of herself, wearing *salwar-kameez*, to make him feel that she is the old Lotus he knew. She has changed and thinks a *sari* may help him to realize it. She has no idea what he wants to say to her, but wonders if he is going to plead about forgiving him and starting over again. Her cell phone rings at seven sharp. It is Bijoy asking if he should come up to get her.

"Don't bother to come up. I will be down," Lotus replies, and even as she is talking over the phone, she is locking up her drawers, putting away her stationary. Then she is ready to leave the office and meet him in the parking lot.

Once outside she sees Bijoy waiting by the entrance of the building. He is wearing a T-shirt and looks relaxed. Before starting the car, Bijoy holds out a rose bouquet to her—yellow roses, her favorite.

He smiles and says, "Yellow roses, right? I hope you still like them. You have changed from a soft girl into a very determined young lady." He pauses. "I know life made you change. It wasn't easy for you. Yes, you have changed a lot."

So, he remembers my favorite flowers, thinks Lotus. But her guard is up, and she knows that, of course, he is trying to win her back. But is it really so easy to win back a broken heart? It is a bit dark inside Sea Food, and Lotus cannot see Bijoy's face clearly. But from what she can make out, he looks happy and carefree, as if just having her with him is making a world of difference for him. She wonders if he really loves her as deeply as he used to. She is surprised to find that she seems to feel happy again with Bijoy. Then she feels guilty as her mind flashes to Adam. She wants to get these confused thoughts over with, and she says, "Look, Bijoy, I came for old time's sake, that is all."

Bijoy frowns at first and then says, "I cannot hold you when I was not here. But now that I am here, I hope things will change and that I will be the only one."

Lotus almost chokes on her the soft drink she was sipping. She thinks: *So, all the pain and humiliation I went through will change just because you appear on your whim?* How he still orders her around. Knowing Adam for the past few days has indeed opened her eyes to how different the two men in her life are. Bijoy is the possessive type, egotistical, and has his own set ideas about life. But Adam is flexible and ready to fall in with other people's ideas if he finds they have merit. It is so easy to talk and move with Adam. It is said that things happens for a reason, and at that moment she is sure that this evening with Bijoy exists only to point out how deeply she now prefers Adam.

Lotus is quiet as her thoughts run around Adam. Bijoy, too, is silent for a while, and then he asks, "Are you worried about something? You are so quiet."

Lotus wakes up from her reverie and hastens to say, "Ah, no, I am not worried. I suppose I am a bit tired, that's all." And then smiling she adds, "The food is good, isn't it?"

After they finish their dinner and order ice cream, Bijoy says, "Shall I count your accepting our date as a new beginning for us, Lotus?

It is Lotus's turn to fall out of the sky. She stares at him disbelievingly before saying, "I agreed because you would not listen to me when I said that I wanted to have nothing to do with you. I didn't want to hurt you and wanted to listen to what you wanted to say." Then looking straight into his eyes she says, "But there is someone else in my life."

"Great! You came just not to hurt me? Don't you see that you still have feelings for me? Otherwise, why would you bother about whether I am hurt or not? This man you are seeing, I know he is divorced and even has a son. You don't want used things, do you?"

Lotus sits, her ice cream melting away. Their simple dinner of shrimp and rice is almost over. She glares at the man in front of her. It is the old Bijoy arguing and acting as if he always knows best. He does not care that she is seeing someone; he does not care about what she wants.

Lotus feels her temper rising. As the waiter taking the bill withdraws, she looks at Bijoy for a long time and then says quietly, "If you are so conscious of my feelings, how come you chose to hurt me? Didn't my feelings mean anything to you then? If you had any clue of how you hurt me, you wouldn't barge in on me like this telling me to forget the past. How dare you tell me who I should spend my life with? I owe you nothing." Lotus is now almost shouting.

"You have changed, Lotus. You would never have been able to say all these things to me a few years ago. But now you are a hard stone. You can say what's on your mind," Bijoy says quietly, as if reprimanding a small child.

Suddenly rising out of his seat, he starts pulling her up from hers. Lotus is not prepared for this, and so when he takes her into his arms and tries to kiss her she is too astonished to react. But recapturing herself she tries to push him away. While they struggle there is a voice saying quietly beside her, "Well, so this is it? Lotus, you are back with your old love?" Adam's gentle voice echoes through her ears.

Lotus gasps. *How can Adam of all people be here?* Bijoy too moves away, hearing the male voice talking to Lotus. Lotus takes a good look at Bijoy, and though she is not sure where she musters the courage, her right hand rises and she slaps him good and hard. She turns to offer Adam some explanations, but by then he has disappeared.

Lotus looks at Bijoy, who is staring at her as if happy to have driven the other man away. She takes her handbag from the table with her left hand and with the right plants another good hard slap on Bijoy's cheek. She has the satisfaction of seeing other diners in the restaurant looking at Bijoy, and one even gives a short laugh, saying, "Bravo, Bangladeshi girls have really come out to save their dignity!"

As Bijoy stands gaping at her, unable to believe what she has done, Lotus storms out the restaurant. She then quickly realizes that it is almost eleven at night and that it is very dangerous for her to be moving alone in the streets of Dhaka. Once out of the door, she checks her cell phone for the number to a taxi service. For some reason she looks up for a moment and freezes. Adam is standing quietly in a corner of the parking lot intently staring at her. But he is not coming to her. It is as if he is not sure of what to do. Lotus just knows that it is she he is waiting for. She rushes toward him and finds his arms are open for her to fall into.

"I don't know, Adam. I don't know why I came. He begged me to come and just listen to what he had to say. It was wrong of me, and I'm sorry, Adam. I'm so sorry."

Lotus sobs as Adam's strong masculine hands hold her to his chest. She feels him holding her tighter as he says simply, "I understand, Lotus. I was waiting for you in case you needed me." He then raises her chin toward his face and Lotus is lost in the deep blueness of his eyes that radiates love even in the dim light of the parking area. "Let's go home," he says as he holds her closely and guides her to his car.

After Adam drops her off at home, Lotus is more confused than ever. *How can Adam be so gentle, understanding, and patient?* He did not show anger, but rather waited to make sure that she was safe after he found her with her old love. Finally Lotus drifts off into a very uneasy sleep not knowing if Adam will still be here for her in the morning.

thirty-six

It is Thursday, the last working day of the week, but Lotus finds herself in no hurry to go home. She decides to visit her mother in the hospital instead. The past few days as she worked in the office, images of her mother have flitted through her mind, as if her mother's soul were calling out to her. She feels a surge of love for the lost soul. Though Lotus does not know it, it *is* in fact Daisy's soul that has been sending messages to Dancing Light, craving love and desiring the closeness of her only child.

Her mother seems to have aged considerably since the last time she saw her. Her hair has become white and wispy, and her skin is as wrinkled as a centenarian's. There is no effort whatsoever on her part to take care of herself. She has no appetite for food, does not wash herself properly, or put on lotions or creams. The hospital seems to overlook taking care of these daily cares that she so desperately needs. Daisy is like an old tree, silently breathing on as storms sweep over her.

"Ma, don't you want to go out with me to see a movie or sit by the lake? Would you like to eat some ice cream?" Lotus asks her on her visit.

Daisy only stares at her balefully, as if those things are little more than a fantasy for her. She then looks at Lotus angrily and hisses, "Why can't you leave me alone? I am happy. Tareq is here with me."

Lotus wonders if her father's spirit does indeed come frequently to her mother. Dancing Light and Daisy's soul comfort the mother and daughter. Dancing Light whispers to Lotus, "I can feel your mother's love for you, for her soul tells me. When you entered the world, she was not the same person. But deep inside, she loves you."

On her way out of the hospital, Lotus looks around and is concerned about the lack of maintenance. Knowing how negligent the authorities are when it comes to holding local hospitals to regulatory standards, Lotus is certain they do not keep up any regular physical exercise for the patients. But what can she do? There are bigger and better hospitals, but she cannot afford them. She has a hard enough time paying the monthly bills of this hospital. Feeling rather depressed she goes home, thinking maybe a visit to Dida might lift her heart after all.

Adam calls during dinner after Lotus arrives home. Lotus can't believe her relief when he doesn't even mention the other night's incident. Her confession and of her confusions seem to stand like a deeper understanding between them. He simply wants to know if she wants to go somewhere over the weekend. He mentions that he has not seen her for some time. Lotus blushes when she realizes that he misses her and that she wants to see him very badly. But she tells him that she does not want to go anywhere on Friday.

To avoid a misunderstanding, she decides to be honest. "I am a bit upset, because of all the happenings with Bijoy, even after that horrible debacle at the restaurant, he is still constantly trying to enter my life again," she tells him. "I have even told him that I am seeing someone, but still he is chasing me around. I just want to be by myself on Friday."

"You can talk about it. I have no problem with it. We can handle it better together. Lotus, you have to clear your own thoughts. You two were together for a long time, and I understand your confusion," says Adam. "Would you like to go out on Saturday instead?"

Hearing his support makes Lotus feel like finding some new ground to stand on. Happily she tells him that she will go out with him on Saturday.

On Saturday, Adam suggests that they visit Daisy. He wants to meet her, he says. He holds her hand and pressing it gently, saying, "I want to share your life as much as I want you to share mine. I am sure I want to see your mother, just as one of these days you will meet my mother. I have told her about you, and she is very happy about us."

On their way to the hospital, Adam buys some oranges and grapes for Daisy. He wishes to buy some flowers, but Lotus has told him that her mother is likely to throw them in his face. One never can tell what her mood will be. Adam buys the flowers anyways and says, "Flowers are symbols of love, and I have to give them to your mother, even if she throws them away."

At the door of the hospital room, with Adam standing by her side, Lotus calls out. "Ma, see who has come to see you."

Daisy is sitting in a chair, and as usual a book is in her hand. She is looking away beyond the window. Hearing her daughter's voice, she puts down the book and stares long and hard at Adam. She rises from her chair, walks toward them, and takes the flowers from his hand. She brings them near her nose and inhales deeply, taking in their fragrance.

Lotus is taken aback. Daisy even holds out her hands for the packets Lotus is holding.

"Ma, are you feeling better?" Lotus asks as she touches her mother lightly on the shoulder.

"There is nothing wrong with me. Why should I not feel well?" asks Daisy, sounding annoyed. Lotus thinks she is dreaming. Her mother responds so easily!

But Lotus realizes that she has asked the wrong question. She knows that people with mental problems usually do not want to be asked about their health, as they tend to be suspicious at times. So changing the subject, Lotus asks, "Ma, do you want to go out in the garden with us?"

She takes the flowers from her mother and puts them on the small table beside the window. As Daisy continues to stare at Adam, he speaks up. "I am Adam, Lotus's friend." Daisy smiles at him. For Lotus, a thousand stars are twinkling in the sky. It's the first time she has ever seen her mother smile. On previous visits, Ma has not even wanted to be in the same room with Lotus, let alone smile at her.

Lotus and Adam lead Daisy through the wide corridor of the hospital into the garden. Daisy walks slowly and hesitantly. Adam goes forward and guides her, firmly holding her right hand. Seasonal flowers are blooming in the small garden. Lotus feels happy as her mother looks around her.

"So many flowers! Why do they keep me inside my room every day? Why don't they bring me out here more often?"

Lotus is astonished that her mother is speaking of her heart's desires. She takes hold of her mother's hands and squeezes them. "Ma, I will tell the nurse to bring you out to the garden more often so that you feel better."

There is a plastic chair under a tree. Lotus asks Ma to sit in it. Daisy sits and sighs deeply, as if feeling content and happy. Lotus settles down cross-legged beside her on the grass. Adam joins her, squatting on the grass beside her.

White jasmines bloom all around the garden. The sweet cloying scent of the flowers fills the air. Adam takes a deep breath, inhaling the fragrance of the flowers, and smiles at Lotus knowingly. They both love jasmine.

A gust of wind sweeps around them and the fragrance of the flowers becomes stronger. Daisy rises and goes near the jasmine tree, lovingly touching each tiny flower. Her whole body seems to be alive with some new life.

Watching her, Lotus feels sad. *Ma must feel like a prisoner. Her heart must be heavy with pangs of loneliness in the confined room of the hospital.* How she wishes that her mother could be like a normal person all the time.

Lotus picks a jasmine flower and holds it toward Daisy. But she can see that Daisy has snapped back to her insanity suddenly. Her eyes are wild and her face looks distorted. Daisy refuses to take the flower from Lotus. Shaking her finger, Daisy says accusingly, "You want to try your witchcraft on me with that flower?" She is almost shouting.

Throwing down the flower, Lotus signals Adam to follow her as she slowly guides her mother back to her room. Unwilling to go inside, Daisy drags her feet. She walks into her room and immediately gets in her bed, looking totally worn out. She lies down with her back to Adam and Lotus, a silent message to go away and leave her alone.

Daisy lies on her bed, her back to the two people who had illuminated her life only a moment before. Adam holds Lotus tightly in his arms before they quietly step out of the room. Lotus knows that in her pain of having a sick mother, she is no longer alone.

thirty-seven

Lotus has put all thoughts of Bijoy from her mind, but it seems the chapter is not over yet. Lotus is watching television and thinking of going to bed early. Just then there is a call from Bijoy. He is in the hospital after a car accident has left him with a broken hand, cuts, and bruises.

"Lotus, please come to see me. I will not ask you ever again. I really want to say sorry in person for all my mistakes."

Lotus knows that he has no one in Dhaka to take care of him. All his relatives live in his hometown of Khulna. Lotus tells him that she will come to see him the next day, since it is night and she does not have a car. Lotus also does not want to be alone when she is with Bijoy, and she asks Chaiti to accompany her the next day. Chaiti agrees but says that she will have to return early as Rajiv is picking her up that afternoon to check out an apartment.

Chaiti and Rajiv's sudden plan to get married in a quiet ceremony last week has wakened Lotus's hidden dreams of having a family. Rajiv, now living with Chaiti in their apartment, is frantically looking for a place where they can make their new home. Lotus teases Chaiti about the sounds of early morning sickness she can hear coming from Chaiti's bathroom, but Chaiti only says, "Didi, love is a strange thing. We cannot always hold on to culture and customs." She then gives Lotus one of those sweet, naughty smiles she keeps specially reserved for special secrets.

On their way to the hospital, they are lucky to find a taxi in front of their home. The streets are full of traffic, and they have a tough time locating the hospital. Dhaka, it seems, is crowded with clinics and hospitals, but when you want to find a particular one, it is easy to become lost in the narrow streets and lanes.

Lotus and Chaiti are worn out by the time they finally locate the small and insignificant looking hospital. They find Bijoy resting after his dinner. Both of his hands are in plaster and small bandages cover various parts of his body.

Lotus and Chaiti are surprised to see a lady wearing a head scarf sitting near his bed. She looks like a Thai or Malaysian woman around thirty years old. She sits there, quiet and demure, like one who knows her place. Lotus notes that she is sitting too close to Bijoy to be a casual acquaintance. The lady smiles at Lotus and Chaiti as they look to her.

"Bijoy, aren't you going to introduce us?" Lotus asks.

Bijoy looks helplessly at the lady. But she rises and says in broken Bangla, "I am Malika, his wife. We were married in Malaysia two years ago."

Lotus gasps with shock but manages to say, "Hello."

Chaiti stares at the woman and then back at Lotus. She says nothing as she shakes hands with Malika. From his bed Bijoy stares, his face scarlet. In his eyes Lotus reads the words of apology he intended to say. At times, silence speaks louder than words.

Lotus, pretending to see none of this, says to Malika, "I am sure you are happy to have a good husband like him. We are just friends who live nearby." Lotus continues to play the good friend as she sits in the chair offered by Malika and says, "Imagine how Bijoy has kept this secret from us. Here he is, married to such a lovely woman, and he did not tell us."

Malika smiles and, running her hands through Bijoy's hair, says, "I understand. He said that his parents would be upset at his marrying a foreigner, but we were so deeply in love. We had a misunderstanding, and he came back to Bangladesh, but here I am back with him. We have a little girl, too, and she is with my mother in Malaysia. Bijoy simply worships our daughter."

Lotus thinks, *Yes, for Bijoy talking of love is easy. Imagine telling me that he is still in love with me while hiding a whole family!* She says to Malika, "You are lovely, and I am sure Bijoy is mad about you," though she is finding it difficult to stay in the same room with Bijoy and his lies.

She thinks of a little girl who is waiting for her father, a father who is chasing his ex-girlfriend around in another country. Lotus hates him and has a whim to slap Bijoy good and hard a third time.

At this moment, Adam's soul touches Dancing Light and tells her very strongly, "See how the Creator holds out truth to Lotus, for she is a good and honest person. And the truth is magnificent. You cannot hide it. Now you have to test the strength of your love for Adam and get her over this shock. You and I can do it together. Tell her repeatedly that Adam is the one who really wants her, go on rewinding all the words and acts of love he has shown her up to now, and keep going until she finds peace and knows that Adam is there for her."

It is Chaiti who manages to hold Lotus's hand before saying good-bye to Malika. Bijoy stares at Lotus from his bed, his eyes imploring her for forgiveness. Adam's soul stops and prays for the Creator to send Tareq's spirit to help Lotus in this crucial time when she is feeling betrayed once again. Dancing Light and Adam's soul begin working in Lotus. They try to bring peace to Lotus's heart as the two see the young ladies suddenly rush out through the door, as if fleeing from a bad nightmare. They hire a three-wheeler and direct the driver to their home. Lotus just wants to be as far away from Bijoy as quickly as possible. Dancing Light can hear Lotus whispering, "Help me, Dad. Help me overcome this bad experience. I am sure your spirit is hovering nearby. Listen to me. Oh, Creator of All, please, help me. Give me the strength to endure."

When Tareq's spirit sees this picture of his daughter calling to him, tears rush down his face.

Dancing Light averts her gaze and says, "Hold on, we are not far from the ending of my tale. When Lotus asked for help, the Creator came to her aid."

Dancing Light then shows Adam how the Creator directs her and Adam's soul to put the light of Adam's love into her, so that she knows she has someone to hold her when she falls.

The Creator puts the seeds of hope into Lotus and sends an angel to help her overcome the pangs of loneliness and deceit. All the way home, Chaiti holds Lotus tightly, feeling her friend's body heaving while she cries silently.

Chaiti hopes that she can find Adam's phone number and call him to come and be with Lotus. Only the hands of love can keep this girl from crumbling after such a shock.

thirty-eight

Back in the apartment, Chaiti asks Lotus, "Didi, do you want me to stay with you?"

But Lotus is composed. For the first time in many years she feels peaceful. Finally, she knows that *not* having Bijoy in her life is a blessing the Creator has given to her. She feels as if her father has been with her all along from Heaven, protecting her. Dancing Light is quick to remind her that, even though Daisy is not in her senses, her heart and soul are constantly praying for her daughter. Lotus smiles at Chaiti and says, "Ah, no, you go ahead and go to sleep. Your husband is waiting for you!"

But Chaiti is worried. She implores, "Didi, shall I call Adam and ask him to come?"

Lotus gives a gentle smile and motions her to go, saying, "Don't worry. Just give me time. I am simply baffled at how we fail to see the inner being of a person because of our own prejudices sometimes!"

As Chaiti opens the door of their room, Lotus can hear soft music and see that the light is still on. Of course, Rajiv is waiting for his wife.

Lotus enters her room and falls onto her bed. It is almost midnight, but she knows she has to call someone. Taking out her cell phone, she pushes Adam's number. "Adam, could you come and hold me in your arms long enough to let me have a good cry? I will tell the guard to let you in."

When Adam hears her voice, he does not ask questions. The urgency is clear to him. It is late for Zuhan, and he is sleeping, but Adam picks up the boy anyway and drives to his mother's place. He looks at his mother's kind face searchingly and says, "Ma, take care of him, and if I am not back tonight, please drop him off at school and pick him up. I will explain later." He just sees his mother nod understandingly before rushing out.

As Adam drives, he can still hear the desperation in Lotus's voice and cannot rest without giving her a call. "Lotus, I am on my way. It will be another ten minutes. Are you okay?"

When Lotus answers, he can tell she has been crying. He wishes he knew some magic to transport him to her side.

Adams stops his car and shuts the door softly. He runs all the way up the stairs after the security guard lets him in. He wishes the building had an elevator.

Lotus opens the door. Adam enters and takes her into his arms. There is no need for words. It is as if both their souls are whispering to each other, "I love you so!"

As soon as their bodies touch, they can feel the warmth between them and something like a magnet drawing them closer and closer. Adam remembers to lock the door. They hold each other tightly, just feeling their love seep into one other. Lotus feels Adam's hands dig into her back until he is almost hurting her. But this pain is delicious. She feels a soft groan escape her lips.

Adam holds her face close to his, and looking deep into her eyes, he asks, "Are you sure, Lotus?"

Lotus looks into his eyes, her own still wet from crying, and she silently nods her head.

"I love you, Lotus. I will always be there for you, as long as I am alive. You won't be alone anymore," Adam says as he holds her tightly and presses her mouth to his, their lips crushed. When his tongue seeks hers, he whispers, "Love, give me your tongue."

"I love you, Adam," Lotus whispers weakly, but she wants him to hear her say it. She does not resist as Adam releases the buttons of her cotton *kameez*. She did not even turn into her night clothes. Lotus's hands go up and around his shoulders, as if to trying to draw him even closer to her. The urgency in his touch matches the rhythm of her hands running up and down his firm back.

Lotus feels her body exploding with a desire she did not know existed in her. She wants Adam to blend into her bare body and wants it as soon as possible. She feels a shiver run through her whole being as Adam's hand slides over to her right breast and softly, ever so softly, clasps it. She feels his fingers linger on her roused nipple. She feels the *kameez* slip to the floor around her bare feet. Her cotton brassiere, already unhooked, slides down her body along with her cotton thong.

Adam guides her to her bed. Lotus clings to Adam with her body. She does not remember him removing his clothes, but he must have done so, for his body is as naked as hers. She clings to him as she has never clung before, not wanting to let go even for an instant. She hears him whisper, "My Lo, I am all yours! I will never leave you." It is as if he can sense the lingering fear of betrayal and loneliness inside her.

Lotus is in tears as Adam's mouth finds her nipples, biting them, sucking them, while his hands explore her naked body. Her own hands are running up and down him, feeling the firm muscles of his shoulders. She closes her eyes as she feels him guiding his manhood into her. There is blazing, delicious warmth as they meet somewhere words cannot describe. No form of communication can express its explicit sweetness! She opens up, and with her hands she urges him to have her completely and forever. As they meet each other on the strong current of love, both pulsating with desire, there is a feeling of being whole, as if finally life holds meaning.

As they lie spent and happy on Lotus's bed, Adam holds her in the circle of his strong arms. He tousles her loose hair so he can smell her shampoo more vividly. There is none of the perfume or incense around them that lovers often use. Both love the sweaty, musty smell of sex and are already feeling as if they want each other again. It is an unspoken agreement. They know that their love is strong enough to endure the forbidden fruit of premarital lovemaking. Love is the intense light they follow, and together they pray that the Creator will be there with them as they follow their hearts.

Adam says, "Well, my queen, I am surprised that you were still a virgin. These days this does not happen with most girls over the age of twenty. Does my being with another woman before bother you?"

Lotus holds him to her bare breasts and whispers, "Adam, it is love that has brought you to me, and I wouldn't care if you had been married twice before as long you still want me now!" Neither Lotus nor Adam is aware of when they fall asleep in each other's arms.

Chaiti is surprised when she sees Lotus's closed door the next morning and concerned, she knocks, "Didi, won't you go to the office? Are you okay?"

Adam and Lotus, waking to the sound of knocking, smile at each other as Lotus says loudly, "No, Chaiti, no office. Adam is with me."

Lotus and Adam hold each other more tightly as they hear Chaiti saying to Rajiv, "Rajiv, I have taught Didi a good lesson in love. She knows now how to cross barriers when she knows she loves someone."

Lotus and Adam both take sick leave from their offices that day, and it is all about Tagore's songs and the Blue Danube playing as they make endless love in the quiet of Lotus's room.

Dancing Light and Adam's souls smile as they watch their hosts caught in the game of love, endlessly amazed at all that goes on in the human world.

thirty-nine

When Lotus misses her period the next month, she is not surprised. In their excitement, neither Adam nor she had thought of taking precautions as they spent long hours in lovemaking. When the pregnancy test is positive, she calls Adam and he says, "Congratulations, my love, and thank you for getting pregnant with our child." She has to whisper for she is sitting in the office and Saima may eavesdrop, the gossiping lady.

"I couldn't be happier, Adam. I feel complete having your child within me," Lotus answers.

Within fifteen minutes, Adam is with her, whisking her out of her seat and making her take an early leave. Next, they are in his apartment, and he is on his knees asking her to be his wife. As they kiss deeply and passionately, he puts a single diamond solitaire ring on her finger.

He says, "Diamonds are not forever, but our love is!"

They have a quiet marriage ceremony. Lotus wears a pale pink wedding gown. She explains to Chaiti, "You know, red is the traditional color for Bangladeshi brides and white is the American one. And so I blended the two to make a pale pink in honor of our mixed parentage." She tells Chaiti of her pregnancy and hears her friend give her own confession. Lotus twitches Chaiti's nose and whispers, "You think your Didi did not understand why you were getting your morning sickness?"

Dida wears pink too and has the longest dance with Adam on the wedding day. She tells her grandson-in-law, "I am sure you are sent by the angels for my Lotus!" Little does she know how true her words are, how the invisible world lights the visible world of the humans!

Soon Lotus and Adam are on their way to the United States. Both of them want their child to be born there. Lotus has already applied for a US visa for Dida, and Abul Uncle will be the one to make sure that she gets on the plane to join them. Zuhan is to be going with them too. Lotus loves the sweet little boy. Lotus feels so happy and fulfilled when the little boy starts to call her "Ma."

Within a few months of living in the United States, Lotus and Adam have managed to bring Daisy and put her in a mental hospital in the next town. Dida has joined them too. Lotus feels so blessed with all the loved ones around her. Seeing the old lady every morning is like watching the sun rise for her. Dida is the embodiment of love in her whole life. She was like the chain that fastened her to life in Bangladesh and now in America, her love surrounds everyone like a heavenly rim. Zuhan has become a great part of her life now. He goes to school. She is there for the boy, through thick and thin.

"Hey, buddy, we are a team and it's our job to make you feel happy. I'm the friend you can always count on me, you know." Lotus sees his face break into a thousand stars every time she says that.

Lotus is glad that she can fulfill Zuhan's dream of having a mother again. Lotus makes sure that Zuhan is by her side all the time. The curly haired little boy with his wide mouth is a carbon copy of his father, and that makes him all the more lovable to her. He is Adam's son, and that is all she cares about. She can hardly wait for the other fruit of their love to join the family.

forty

Back in North Carolina, Lotus has to go through some legal matters before she can gain possession of a small house her grandmother left for her in Ashville. Dancing Light and Adam's souls are happy, and they are already in touch with the soul that the Creator has put in Lotus's womb. Dancing Light has heard Lotus and Adam discussing a return to Bangladesh after the child is born; they want to be fair to their Bangladeshi family, after all. Dancing Light wants to time travel and see the future of the unborn child, but the Creator will not allow her to.

She hears the Creator's voice come to her. "You have to leave some matters to me. I will decide when the child will be born and what destiny this child, a girl, will hold. You see, though I have brought Lotus and Adam together, I still have not planned how long they will be together in life and death's dance."

Dancing Light and Adam's soul are busy guiding their hosts. Adam and Lotus feel anxious whenever they take the highway while driving. The accident that took away Tareq haunts them.

Adam's soul says, "These poor humans. They have such unpredictable futures, and the two things they want in this short life is to live long and to be happy. Yet those two things are given by the Creator at his will. Happiness and long life cannot be guaranteed, despite all the science and arts they develop."

"Do you think the Creator will punish Adam and Lotus for their love child? I mean, sex is supposed to come after the marriage vows ideally," Adam's soul asks Dancing Light.

"I suppose Lotus and Adam care little about the consequences as long as they have each other. You see, love makes human beings blind to everything. And love also brings out the best of one's being and takes humans beyond religion and race. I know that they will ask for forgiveness to the Creator and He is always there for his creations."

"Love, it is magic, isn't it? Dancing Light, you know I have fallen in love with you?" Adam's soul asks.

"And I love you too," says Dancing Light. "But that is the forbidden fruit for us. We make our hosts fall in love, but we are to remain unattached." They look at each other helplessly.

They hear the Creator's voice saying, "Though you are sent to create love and contentedness in humans, you are not to fall in love with each other. I do not want you to suffer, for you will return to me but as your individual selves. Even in the Land of Illumination, your life is temporary. I may bring ends to both, this and the human world, at any moment."

※

At this very moment, Adam and Lotus are sitting on the sandy beach of Wilmington. It is a beautiful summer day. As the sea waves crash on the shore and wash over their bare feet, Lotus feels as if her father's spirit is with them, watching and cautioning them. She feels the first butterfly movements of the unborn child in her womb. The white clouds sail lazily in the blue sky, and the rows of pine trees along the shore sway gently as if agreeing with her. Dancing Light and Adam's soul are busy looking after the new soul in Lotus. The new soul in Lotus's womb trembles with excitement.

Dancing Light wonders what Lotus is going to name her child, what kind of life she will have? *Life,* she thinks, *is a mystery indeed.* Suddenly Dancing Light wants to go back to the Land of Illumination. She wants to be with other souls. But she wants to be with Adam's soul too. She wants to be with him as long as she can. How did she get caught up in this game of love, and what will happen to them now? She cannot stop her feelings for him.

She pokes Adam's soul. "Hey, buddy, how did we get entangled in our mission to bring our hosts together? Why is this love thing so crazy?"

She only hears a chuckle in response and knows that like her he has no answer. Life for Lotus, Adam, and the new soul in Lotus's womb are all tests of life, and the future hangs in the balance, as unpredictable as ever. Dancing Light hears the Creator's message: "Humans do not know what lies around the corner of the future."

In the invisible world, the Creator smiles and puts His words of wisdom into those who believe in His superior force. Science, art, music, history, geography, and astronomy, name only a few of the thousands things that hold life with their forces. Who is at the helm of it all? It is the Creator who reveals the secrets of life when he chooses. He hides facts to baffle humans and have them chasing the mysteries of the visible and invisible.

Part Seven

Horizon Day—II

Dancing Light and Entrance of Yet Another Soul

forty-one

It is Horizon Day again and Dancing Light is done showing the story of Lotus's life in Bangladesh for Tareq's spirit. The spirit thanks her as they gather along with other invisible beings. Lotus's pregnancy is nearing full term. The new soul inside her is excited, as Dancing Light keeps her updated about life in North Carolina.

As the souls gather, the new baby's soul asks Dancing Light to take her to the souls' party. Dancing Light smiles and says, "Look, any moment the Creator will be sending his message to have you out into the world. You'll join us once you are born. I can see you are going to be one hell of a party girl, already dancing and wanting to go out to meet others!" Dancing Light gives a playful tug on the unborn baby's nose. That makes the baby give a kick, and Lotus puts a gentle hand on her big belly to comfort her baby. She is waiting for the baby, waiting to take admission in the hospital any moment.

Meanwhile, the invisible beings—the souls, spirits, angels, and genies—are having this sudden meeting in the human world in celebration of the new soul that is coming through Lotus. Dancing Light came through some very challenging situations when she was born, and the other souls had been apprehensive about her whole life. But the new soul with Lotus is to be born with a star shining on her head. Lotus holds on to the goodness of her heart, no matter how difficult life becomes, and she has not wronged or hurt others knowingly. In reward the Creator is giving her a wonderful child to love and cherish. No gift can be greater than love.

Leaving Lotus asleep, Dancing Light has come to join the souls' gathering. At the meeting Dancing Light informs the other souls of what she has seen. "I was allowed to time travel for Lotus's baby, and I see a wonderful life ahead. She will contribute to the human world with a unique medicine that may be like a vaccination to cancer!"

Adam's soul sitting near her pats her on the back and says, "Perhaps finally the humans will find a cure for this deadly disease. I'm glad we were able get Lotus and Adam together."

On this Horizon Day, other souls are also busy gathering information about guiding their hosts. At this moment all the souls have left their hosts in the hearts' hands; the hearts beat on in the sleeping hosts, but the souls are out here together enjoying the party.

Dancing Light tells Tareq's spirit, "Look, I am already worried about the Land of Illuminations where I will go when Lotus's life is over. Will I get her favorite food up there? Will she have her cheese pizza, her rice pudding, songs she cannot live without? Will she have her favorite books or be connected to Facebook?"

Tareq's spirit smiles gently. The spirits understand the confusion within human minds, hearts, and souls. "Well, the physical needs end with death. She will definitely not have the worldly goods: the house that one cannot do without, the bank account that one slaves to fill, the social status people kill themselves for. None of these will go beyond their existence on Earth. But the Creator will fulfill all desires with things invisible. For people who lead good lives, He gives them a sense of fulfillment so they feel content as death takes over and peace follows their returning souls."

Tareq's spirit feels a tug from the Creator. He has to go but cannot without giving a last piece of advice to Dancing Light. Before he starts to fly away, he has just time to say, "It's the heart that does much work in life. It has another meaning to humans. In their hearts they love or hate. They accept and reject life's wants and needs, but it is their heart that has to be guarded at all times."

Dancing Light sighs. The battle ahead seems to be tougher as Lotus's life is joined to Adam, Zuhan, and the new soul in Lotus's womb.

"Hello there, Dancing Light!" comes the cry of a soul sitting a little distance away.

Dancing Light turns to see the soul of Dennis, the soul she met on Facebook. Dancing Light asks him, "I remember you told me about your love for an angel. How is it going?"

"I am still living, you know, and so the angel comes by and I get to see her. But when my host dies, I suppose that will be the end. No romance in the Land of Illumination, you know. Humans may have happy love affairs, but for us invisible beings it seems to be always tragic love," sighs Dennis's soul.

"Hey, I can hear orders to return immediately to Lotus. She is having her baby!" Dancing Light suddenly shouts and in a moment disappears. Other invisible beings carry on their discussion of the human world. An angel joins them.

A soul who is sitting quietly near the angel speaks up. "I belong to a sex worker. She is a pretty lady with a good heart. The work she does is not liked by others in society. I feel so sorry at times when she falls in love momentarily with her clients. When she takes in a client, the brain is the one that counts the dollars but at times the heart lingers. It longs to hear a word of real love, though she knows well the client is only saying words that mean nothing!"

Another soul feeling sorry says, "I belong to a sage and my host is like a flower inside, all pure and goodness. He wants to help people all the time. Maybe he can guide a man to her and help her find real love."

A tinkle of laughter comes from the back while another soul enters the debate. "My host is a doctor. She checks her patients and sends them to specialists. I hear her surprise when she finds so many men and woman coming in with sex-related diseases. At times the humans invite so much trouble, all for sex."

All the souls stare at another who says, "Without these strange combinations of human beings, my host would be out of her livelihood. She is a journalist and looks for the ingredients of her work among people. Journalists find strange stories in real life from all walks of life!" The prim little soul sitting on a tree, enjoying the breeze, says.

It is time for all the souls to return from their meeting on Horizon Day. Dancing Light has just come back after the delivery of Lotus's baby. All the invisible beings rejoice the entrance of another soul into the human world. They assure Dancing Light of their support with looking after her host's baby.

Dancing Light prepares to go back to Lotus. The meeting of the invisible beings is closing and Horizon Day is at an end. The souls flutter around each other, seeking their ways back to their hosts. They have no regrets about how much or how little they have accomplished this day. All beginnings have endings and so does this day. Dancing Light speeds up her flight to Lotus. But suddenly all souls are aware of a new arrival.

There is a tremor in the breeze, and they hear a soft new voice say, "Hi, souls, I'm Prancing Light, just born and my host is Lotus. From today onwards, all souls are getting a new name. I heard a voice called "The Creator" giving me this message." The soul pauses as if in doubt and then goes on. "But what does my Creator look like, and where will I find him? An angel guided me to your meeting here."

All the souls are shaken. The name they have all shared for so long is to change? They want to be sure there has been no mistake.

"Are you sure, Prancing Light? All souls born from today will share the name of Prancing Light in the Land of Illumination?"

As the new soul nods her head in consent, Dancing Light tries to find a solution to the sudden change. "It seems that humans want to move with so much speed these days that the Creator has given the souls a new name from this day, prancing as a movement relates to faster speed than dancing."

As Lotus's soul is asking where she can find the Creator again, Dancing Light says, "The Creator is invisible, and we the souls too are invisible. But we find the Creator in all his creations, the whole universe, and beyond. We, the souls in our human hosts and other living things are glaring examples of His existence."

Prancing Light gives a soft laugh but in a wondering voice says, "On the journey of life to find my Creator, I wonder what mysteries wait ahead!"

Dancing Light extends her hand to Prancing Light saying, "Come, we must get you back to your host. She is waking up from her first sleep in the human world. But know that on your journey you are not alone. So long as the human world survives, we are in it together, buddy."

Prancing Light, curious like the whole generation of her kind, speaks up again, "How long will the human world last?"

"All are in the hands of the Creator. We are the lives that come and go on His wheel of eternity. You have long way to go, child. You have long way to go."

The End

Tulip Chowdhury is a freelance writer and retired teacher whose work has previously appeared in newspapers and magazines. Chowdhury's previous publications include collections of poems (*The Raindrops and Nature and Love*), short stories (*Stars in the Sky*), essays (*Reaching Beyond Words*) and a compiled work of fiction, poetry, and essays (*Rainbow*). Her latest work of fiction, Visible, Invisible and Beyond, and a poetry collection, "*Red, Blue, Purple*" are now available.

Made in United States
North Haven, CT
24 October 2022